Anonymous

The Pauliad

An Epic Poem

Anonymous

The Pauliad
An Epic Poem

ISBN/EAN: 9783337401573

Printed in Europe, USA, Canada, Australia, Japan

Cover: Foto ©Andreas Hilbeck / pixelio.de

More available books at **www.hansebooks.com**

THE

PAULIAD;

AN

EPIC POEM.

TO WHICH

HIS ROYAL HIGHNESS THE PRINCE OF WALES

HAS MOST GRACIOUSLY PLEASED TO BECOME

A SUBSCRIBER.

PUBLISHED BY JOHN MAXWELL AND COMPANY,
122, FLEET STREET.

———

MDCCCLXIII.

Price Tea Shillings.

THE PAULIAD

OR

THE LAST DAYS

OF

THE GREAT APOSTLE

TO THE

GENTILES.

An Epic Poem.

PART THE FIRST.

IN SIX BOOKS.

To

George M. Lord Lyttelton,

With an enduring sentiment of

ADMIRATION

for that galaxy of Talent that illuminated our Literary Hemisphere during the

first half of the last Century,

where the

Name or Star of LYTTELTON shines with more than ordinary lustre;

and with a grateful remembrance of

His Lordship's early Patronage and familiar intercourse,

This small but sincere Tribute of Respect and Esteem

is

by permission inscribed,

By the AUTHOR.

PREFACE.

When an unknown author assumes the dress of a Poet and braves the Public ordeal, nothing is, or perhaps ought to be, set down in extenuation of his temerity. Still, should this little production be suffered to pass into notice, some explanation is due, and may be necessary, as well to conciliate the impartial but lenient judgment of the reader as to deprecate the chastisement of the critic.

It is now some years since the first book or canto of the present production saw the light in the shape of a Poem generally known as the Prize Poem. The author, then residing at Cambridge, though in no way connected with the University, heard with surprise the almost unprecedented decision of the authorities—that no prize, or medal (the Chancellor's medal) annually given, would that year be awarded.

It was generally understood, whatever might have been implied, that there was no Poem good enough; whereupon the author, actuated by motives that it is unnecessary and would be difficult to recall or explain, immediately applied himself to the task of supplying the deficiency, and, at the instigation of perhaps too partial friends, made his maiden attempt known through the Press.

The circulation was confined principally to the University, town, and county of Cambridge, and the neighbouring county of Norfolk; but the reception it met with from Noblemen, Gentlemen, and others, some of them distinguished for their learning and standing at the University, was as generous as it was flattering; and the author, ever cherishing a lively remembrance of it, and conceiving the subject capable of extension, has at different times penned the additional books, which are now for the first time published together as the first part of an Epic Poem.

More need not be said: therefore, with the forlorn hope that this crude production, unworthy as it is of the Title and the sublime Visions it has so faintly reflected, may be the means of reviving a love for the Classic Muse and an emulation of her votaries — the very semblance of whose works are overshadowed by those of a lighter texture—and of stimulating the minds of others who, with a purer conception, a more lofty imagination and a more enlightened capacity, combine easy circumstances, tranquil leisure, and contemplative habits, to endeavour to restore this portion of our literature, which the tastes of the present day tend so evidently to neglect or disparage, the author with trembling heart and hand submits his efforts to the judgment of a just, a liberal, and discerning Public.

ERRATA.

Page 163, Note n, for "Tautus" read "Tacitus."

Page 164, Note n, for "Taut. *Ann.*" read "Tacit. *Ann.*"

Page 165, Note r, for "Lastantius" read "Lactantius."

BOOK I.

—

PAUL AT ROME;

OR,

THE BURNING OF ROME BY NERO.

———◆———

ARGUMENT.

The Poem opens with the conflagration of Rome. Nero instigated by crime and ambition resolves on setting fire to the city, which he views from Mecænas' tower—Collects his slaves and imparts his resolution to them—Their Satanic joy—He leaves the palace in disguise at their head—Is arrested by the sound of music—Its power over him—Is addressed by a female, whom he accompanies to a midnight assembly of people of both sexes and all ranks and nations—They sing a hymn to God—His wonder at their mixed character, strange appearance and new mode of worship—Recognizes many whom he had known—At length he discovers St. Paul, who addresses the meeting —Nero, enraged at his discourse utters a loud cry, and rushing to the door joins his menials and immediately commences the work of devastation—The meeting disperse—Their forebodings—The eruption of Mount Vesuvius—The first appearance of the fire—Its rapid increase and its horrors—Ancient monuments destroyed—The misery of the inhabitants — The soldier and the sailor — Despair — Final triumph of Nero.

THE BURNING OF ROME.

Of God's chief-chosen instrument to bring
Man to the knowledge of the truth I sing :
Of him whose faith and energy combined,
Wrought wondrous changes in the human mind :
Whose fervent zeal and toilsome travel spread
Revealed religion : and the Gospel sped
'Mongst heathen nations ; hitherto immersed
In darkness deep ;—whose idols he dispersed—
Gave to the winds their mythologic lore,
Made them with him the one true God adore :
Subverted systems ; worship introduced,
Before unknown—and by his works produced
New thoughts, new hopes, new motives and new rules,
That put to shame the wisdom of the schools :
Exalted human nature to its bounds,
Till with his fame the universe resounds :
His trials, visions, woes while I indite,
Come, inspiration, aid me to recite !

When ' Rome's sixth Emperor' the sceptre swayed,
And half the world his single nod obeyed ;

When the Imperial city groaned beneath
His tyrant arm, and the triumphant wreath
Bound not the victor's, but the murderer's brow ;
When power's quenchless lust had made him now
A sanguinary demon, and he trod
On human law, and thought himself a god :—
When crime on crime had every tie bereft,
And to his monster's heart no more was left ;
Not e'en a friend to die at his command,
Nor kindred blood to saturate his hand ; [a]
Then did his soul a deed sublime conceive,
Surpassing all in guilt, yet should retrieve
His blackened name, to after ages leave
(However gods may curse, or men may blame)
A lasting monument of Nero's fame.

    Mecænas' tower he climbed ; thence he saw [b]
Masses of shapeless buildings, without order, law,
Form, or uniformity, together heaped
As if from out of chaos they had leaped ;
With no directing genius to control
The builder's rude designs, or to unroll
To their untutored minds the scanty page
Of science, destined for an after age.
Long winding streets, and narrow noisome ways,
On each and all sides met the Emperor's gaze ;
The refuge of the bad from every clime,
The stye of pestilence, the sink of crime :
Temple and fane of fair proportion shorn,
Column and arch by time and tempest worn,

Palaces and prisons together hurled,
Unworthy of the Mistress of the World.
He saw, and he resolved—so foul a stain
On Cæsar's rule no longer should remain ;
Ambition fired his heart, and he resolved,
With impulse dire, that Rome should be involved
In one stupendous ruin. He thought not, he,
Of all the woe, the death, the misery,
Upon his fellow-beings he should bring ;
His thoughts were soaring on the golden wing
Of future grandeur ; when there should arise
Another city, whose beauty should surprise,
Surpass all men's conceptions, and become
The Empire's pride, the new, the splendid Rome.

Descending then, he hastened to impart
This monstrous purpose of his wicked heart,
To his most trusty slaves ; men whom he knew,
Remorseless, reckless, ready to imbrue
Their hands in blood ; those slaves who had before
To victims oft his cruel mandates bore :
Hardened by crime, in every kind of strife ;
For action fierce, with hope of plunder rife.
How did their eyes with tiger's fury glare !
How did their tongues with savage joy declare
Their will to execute his dire command,
And at his beck, to ply the fiery brand !
As Satan stood amid his rebel host,
On the wild waves of fierce ambition lost ;

To further deeds of guilt exhorting all,
Burning with anguish at their recent fall :
So Nero stood, surrounded by his slaves,
And he to be the chief of demons craves ;
Commands them all to spare nor sex nor age,
If any dare prevent, or stop their rage ;
But without mercy to consume, destroy,
And make Imperial Rome another Troy.

In deep disguise he left the palace gate,
And his vile slaves upon his footsteps wait :
Incendiaries all, on devastation bent,
Fit to fulfil their bloody chief's intent :
Each bore a torch, and each was well supplied
With igneous matter, from Vesuvius' side.[d]
'Twas midnight now, an awful stillness reigned ;
Sleep's soft but powerful duress had enchained
The poor devoted city, ere she fell
An easy conquest to these sons of hell.
Onward they pressed until they reached the site
Where Cœlius and Palatinus unite ;[e]
Where the Great Circus, with combustion stored,
Did a full field for their design afford.
But mark :—their leader stops, he waves his hand ;
In sudden silence stop the villain band ;
Wondering that aught his purpose could arrest,
What unseen power his mind had now possessed :
Listening he stands under some strange control,
Fixed like a statue in the Capitol.

The soft sweet cadence of the matchless lute,
The reed's shrill sound, harmonious, though acute—
The spirit-stirring harp has caught his ear;
And music's charms to him were ever dear:
In earlier years, ere vice had yet possessed
Complete dominion o'er his youthful breast,
He woo'd and won the muses; chief of all
Her who had power the senses to enthral,
To exorcise the demon from the heart,
Like a magician's spell to set apart,
Allay the evil passions for a time,
And bind the soul in ecstacy sublime.

As thus he stood, in silent rapture lost,
Who dare approach, who dare their lord accost?
A female voice has summoned him away;—
No word he spoke but motioned them to stay;
Then on those wondering minions turned his back,
And closely followed on the maiden's track.
" Come, let us haste, my sire will for us wait;
" And at such times 'tis sin to be too late."
These words fell softly from the stranger's tongue,
As now with hurried step she passed along;
He followed her, he knew not why nor where,
For still the spell that bound his thoughts was there.
Through dark and narrow paths she led the way,
To where the more distinct and louder play
Declared the spot from whence those sounds arose,
That almost went his purpose to transpose:

And here the stranger stopt, and gently tapt,
And gave a signal; in his cloak he wrapt
His well-known face, though darkness and disguise
Had veiled his features from her guileless eyes.

They passed the entrance of a spacious store
With tapers lit around, while on the floor
Assembled hundreds stood;—he left his guide,
And quick behind the crowd contrived to glide,
Till he had reached a station near the wall,
Unknown to her, and unperceived by all:
For in delightful harmony arise
In slow and solemn accents to the skies,
Worship and praise, with dulcet notes combined,
To God, the greatest tribute of mankind:
Full on his ear the vocal concert rung,
And these the words, and this the song they sung. "

I.

Great God of all things! who can bid arise
The weaker vessel to confound the wise;
Let Thy pure spirit in our hearts abide;
That we may be fit instruments to guide,
From ignorance and idle worship those
Repentant sinners, whom all climes enclose,
To the true knowledge of Thy holy word,
Jesus our Master, Saviour, King and Lord.

II.

If bonds, or death, or persecution wait
Us. Thou hast chosen to disseminate
The blessed doctrines of Thy Gospel light.;
Oh! fortify our hearts, that we may fight
The fight of faith; and in the trying hour,
Condemned to suffer by some earthly power,
Then may we on Thy promises rely,
Like Jesus pardon, and like Jesus die.

The song had ceased: with wonder he surveyed
The strange assembly that was there displayed:
He saw no God to whom the people prayed,
No Œdile there in gorgeous vest arrayed;
No sacrifice, with garlands to attire,
No vestal virgins with the sacred fire:
Each sex, all ranks, all nations, there were met,
Without distinction, without order set:
As in the great last day, when summoned all,
To plead in person at our Maker's call;
When earthly honours into nothing fade,
And all before Him are of equal grade:
So even here, ambition is forgot,
Noble or artizan, whate'er their lot,
In common supplicate, in common stand,
Merging distinction in one common band.

Erect, and known to Nero by his style,
Stood Sergius Paulus, late from Cyprus Isle,

Returned Proconsul;' kneeling by his side
The lovely fair one that had been his guide:
Her head upraised, her fixed yet beaming eye
(And which to him seemed bent on vacancy):
Her arms too, crossed upon her virgin vest,
Denote the inward feelings of her breast,
To be to heaven directed; emblem she,
Of purest faith and true humility:
Who bends o'er her, with melancholy brow ?
The young Valerius; well he knew him now,
The fond associate of those halcyon days
When nought but innocence the mind displays:
And well he knew his sire's untimely fate,
Condemned to death by Messalina's hate.ʲ
His anxious look, and sometimes vacant stare,
Pronounced that he too was a stranger there:
What thoughts did not the sight of him recall!
'Twas but a moment, but in that moment all
Their early years, the other's spotless course,
His own career of crime without remorse,
Flashed on his mind: then did the scorpion's sting
Enter his soul, and to his senses bring
The vastness of the gulph that lay between
The good and bad;—by him before unseen,
Now made impassable:—transient was the thought,
And his fell soul, with further evil fraught.

Others there were of Senatorian rank,
Who at this font of simple worship drank:

Philosophers he saw, of either sect,
And among the rest he could detect
The far-famed Dionysius,[k] at whose school
Of attic eloquence he learned the rule;
Tribunes, Centurions, Legionaries too,
' And honourable women not a few:'
In native guise reclining on the floor,
The painted Briton and the tawny Moor;
Strangers from climes, where'er the Roman name
Had yet been carried, to the assembly came

But there were three whom Nero now observed
Distinct in figure, by design preserved
Apart from all; and on their presence hung
The strange desire with which all hearts were strung.
The first was of a tall majestic form,
In Esculapian garb;[l] on his right arm
Leant one of smaller stature: in whose face
And form attenuated they might trace
The lineaments of age and mental strife:
Anguish and woe that wait upon a life
Of self-denial: zeal, anxious love,
Enthusiastic labour to disprove,
Dispel the clouds of error, that enshrined
God's great, sublimest work—the human mind
Close on his right, a legionary stood,[m]
With folded arms, as if in thoughtful mood:
His eyes were fixed—the Esculapian's too,[n]
On him betwixt them; but the anxious view

Of love, solicitude, and tender care,
Evinced the wish the latter had to share
In all his sorrows;—while the soldier's gaze
Was one of supplication and amaze.

Advancing from between them he displayed
A massive chain;[o] the sudden sound betrayed
Enough at once for Nero to recall
The care-worn features of the prisoner Paul,
By Portius Festus from Judæa sent,
To him appealing for enfranchisement;
But no, his wicked heart had twice denied
Justice to him, who twice his power defied:
Twice had he quailed beneath that scorching look,
Twice upon his justice seat he shook,[p]
When Paul in terms emphatic and severe,
Upheld his cause, denouncing without fear,
The Gentile Gods, and Jewish unbelief;
Declaring, proving, from the Scripture leaf,
Jesus, whom Pilate crucified, was He
Who lived and reigned from all eternity.

When from before the glorious orb of day,
The mists are wafted suddenly away;
Then his effulgence more than ever seems,
His brightness then with greater splendour beams:
'Twas so with Paul, when stretching forth his hands,
A heavenly halo o'er his face expands;
A brighter lustre from his eye there broke,
As he with god-like inspiration spoke:—[q]

" Brothers and men, and all assembled here,
" Mark what I say, and hold my counsel dear :
" The God I serve, the Lord in whom I trust,
" To those blessed mansions where abide the just,
" Will shortly call me : my ministry is done,
" And I the course assigned to me have run.
" Twice as you know, before that man of blood,
" I've been arraigned, and twice his rage withstood :'
" But now, the Spirit tells me from within,
" The reign of persecution will begin ;
" Satan has ta'en possession of his mind,
" And burns to wreak his vengeance on mankind :
" Terror and death unite with him, t'assail,
" The Church of God ; but they shall not prevail :
" Constancy and endurance must defeat
" Their utmost efforts, and their tortures meet.
" Soldiers of Christ be firm ; hold fast the faith :
" Sin not ;—remember what our Master saith :
" ' He who his life for my Name's sake does give,
" ' In everlasting happiness shall live :'
" Tongue cannot tell nor mortal can conceive,
" The bliss prepared for those that do believe.
" Fear not the lion," he has no power to harm,
" Save what is given him by the Almighty's arm ;
" This life he may destroy, but cannot kill
" The souls of those who seek to do His will.
" This monstrous demon whom He now permits,
" And who such gross enormities commits,
" Is but an instrument, Christ's name to spread,
" Feared but by those who in his footsteps tread.

" At all times then, and in all places, preach
" Jesus crucified, and his gospel teach :
" In prayer be constant, and in praise be loud :
" Exhort the humble, and rebuke the proud :
" That when our last account He shall require,—
" When this wide world shall be consumed by fire,"—

 " Let that be while I live then ;"—Nero cried ;—
A thrill of horror—when the crowd espied
His fiendish features—all their senses bound,
While she,— his guide,—fell speechless to the ground :
Like thunder's awful burst his voice had dealt
Tumultuous fear around—sudden she felt
Herself the cause of every future ill
That must befal—herself unconscious still :
That pang of self-reproach that none can tell,
Struck on her heart like a demoniac's spell,
One piercing shriek escaped her and she fell.
While with a mind to utmost frenzy wrought
He reached the portal, and his minions sought ;
At hand he found them, they too had been lured,
To near the spot, where he had just endured
Those pangs of conscious guilt, that ne'er are cured :
Where he had writhed, beneath the lash of one,
Whose mean estate, contrasted with his own
Power and pride had taught him to despise ;
Yet there was something he could not devise,
Somewhat in the prisoner's speech and mien,
Surpassing all he e'er before had seen ;

Awed by a power, his spirit could not brook
With inward passion, every fibre shook
And evil spirits must at some time cower,
Before the throne of justice, truth and power:
So Satan felt, when the Archangel's sword,
Which he had wielded at the Almighty's word,
Met the revolting chief's, and cleft his side;
Then shame and rage, and disappointed pride,
Increased the anguish he could not suppress,
Though 'twere a greater anguish to confess.

In such a mood he called his slaves around
And to the pitch of utmost fury wound
Their hellish spirits; whom he thus addressed,
Paul's withering words still on his mind impressed :—
" No more delay, your torches now ignite,
" My rage these base born Christians shall requite;
" Haste to your work, let nothing now retard,
" That work destruction, plunder your reward;
" Let them receive no mercy at your hands,
" Who dare dispute the Emperor's commands."
Too well obeyed, he snatched a lighted torch,
And quick applied it to the nearest porch;
To heap on fuel some attendants came,
While others stooped to fan the infant flame."

Within, what dread—what consternation dwelt!
The sorrowing damsels round their sister knelt;
First raise her helpless form, then try the test
Of such appliance as their minds suggest:

Her hands they chafe, her temples bathe and press
Her livid lips, while wailing forth distress :—
But chief her sire and young Valerius moan
Her helpless fate, and answer groan for groan.
" Oh speak, Paulina—to thy allianced speak " —
Silent her tongue, like marble was her cheek—
" Alas ! she breathes not ; whose grievous fault is this—
" Valerius—how ?" imprinting then a kiss
On her cold brow, the sire appealed to Paul
Who wrapt in love, these soothing words let fall :—
" Restrain your grief—this sickness is not death
" Life will return, and breath succeed to breath,
" Luke the beloved physician will impart
" His instant care and tender all his art :
" Take comfort to your hearts this maid shall live
" And of her faith a further proof must give—
" See even now, her lips—her nostrils move—
" Retire and shield her with a Christian's love :
" Remember Him, whom I pronounce as true,
" He will preserve, who died for us and you."

Meanwhile both men and women issue fast
From out the store, not heeding as they passed,
The conflagration that had scarce commenced,
For the select incendiaries were fenced
By other slaves, with torches held on high
To watch their motions as the crowd passed by :
And some there were of Nero's household too
A long time members of the Christian crew,

Who by the torches' glare could well descry
Their fellow slaves ; but to what purpose, why
Assembled there, at such unusual time,
Unless to perpetrate some hideous crime
They could not tell ; and homeward as they went
All marvelled greatly at the dire portent.

The cloud that capt Vesuvius," ere the blaze
Burst from her summit, hovering many days,
Did not more truly to the plains foretell
The desolation that on them befell ;
Sweeping, destroying Man's abode and Man.
Effacing Nature's marks—Art's finest plan:
Then did these congregated demons shew,
The near forthcoming of some fatal blow,
The sure forerunner of some mighty woe :
Not long before the dawn alarm was given,
And with redoubled cries the air was riven ;
The sky, before so beautifully clear,
Now when the night began to disappear,
Was not illumined with that cheering ray,
Those ambient tints, that mark the coming day :
That cause the heart to bound, the mind to soar,
In gratitude above, and God adore ;
But with a murky glow, a lurid glare,
That sunk the soul in sadness and despair :
Above, the smoke volume o'er volume curled,—
Below, the flames death and destruction hurled
On all around : assisted by the winds,
Their fury knows no bounds, no respite finds :

To stop their progress, vain was human aid,
Vain the attempt, by whomsoever made ;—
For Nero's mandates were so well observed,—
So well those demons of their chief deserved,
That none dare offer to impede their course ;
And they increased with such resistless force,
The Circus soon one burning pile became,
Her stores and dwellings, one continuous flame.

Who shall describe the horrors that ensued ?
With heart of steel the Muse should be endued—
A mind attuned to woe, to contemplate,
E'en through the lapse of ages, and relate
That dreadful tale of danger and distress,
That vast amount of human wretchedness ;
Death here was met in his most hideous form :
No hope of rescue, when the first alarm
Aroused them all from labour's sweet repose ;
Men, wives and children, who their eyes did close,
In confident security, awake,
All hapless, helpless, hopeless,—and forsake
Their scorching couch—around, above, below,
They see—nought but destruction, and they know
At once their doom ;—from all sides then arise
The piercing shrieks, the agonizing cries
Of wild despair ; until the thundering sound
Of falling ruins, every other drowned.

Yes, Death unsparing, unrelenting Death,
Havoc has made of hundreds in a breath ;

No requiem sung, no mourners there the while,
Their homes, their substance, made their funeral pile;
But with the Circus' fall, their sufferings ceased:
Not so the flames—to giant strength increased,
They, like the boiling lava, overcome
The walls of prisons, and the palace dome;
Altar and fane, that ages consecrate;
Old works of art, that all most venerate;
Trophies obtained, in many a well fought field;
Proud genius' store, and literature yield
To their devouring fury;—all is gone
That time and science, blood and conquest, won.'
Nor did Rome's guardian deity escape;
Jove's temple now reminds them of the rape
The poet fabled had occurred of old,
When he descended as a shower of gold
In Danäe's lap: lo! now they may behold
The temple's ruins, smoking on the ground,
And glittering sparks that fill the air around.²

Six times the sun had risen, six times had set,
Unheeded on the city; for as yet
Despair and death—destruction and dismay—
Made it to them one long continued day;
Or one dread night of aggravated woe;
For human misery had fall'n so low,
Some would a voluntary death embrace,
Upon the very spot, or near the place,
Where their paternal home in ruins lay;
Or where their early days, in youthful play

Had passed; where by industrious arts they earned
Their daily bread; their implements now burned,
They, in their desolation left alone,
Sought not to live, when means to live were gone.
Others would struggle harder with their fate,
Eager to rescue some endearing mate,
An aged parent, or a much loved child,
Who in their haste they left;—now frantic, wild
With fear and love, returned among the dead,
And braved the danger they before had fled.
The strong exhort the weak—the weak bewail
No chance of safety;—then the strongest quail:
Wringing their hands in bitterest woe they lie—
Cursing their gods in heaps despairing die.

The soldier meets his foe upon the plain,
Determined he to conquer or be slain;
With ardour warm, his generous bosom burns;
In hope of conquest, fear of death he spurns;
Fighting he falls, and when to upper air
His spirit flees, he never knows despair.
The shipwrecked sailor climbs from rock to rock—
Impending dangers all his efforts mock;
Still he has hope—the hope that bad him brave;
Buffet with lusty arm the threatening wave
And bid defiance to a watery grave,
Still helps him on—dashed from a point he falls,
Dies on the spot, and no despair appals.

Thou elder born of sorrow and of sin,
In Hell begotten, nurtured 'mong the din
Of howling demons; with perpetual pains
Destined to struggle in eternal chains;
Servant of Satan, here assume thy sway;
Triumph Despair—rejoice—exult—survey
Thy countless victims; absolute thy will,
Of human wretchedness, here glut thy fill.

And where was he who all this evil made?
High on the tower where lately he surveyed
The lofty city and the busy crowd,
He stood; and with satanic joy endowed,
Unmindful of the dead, and dying groans
Of hapless wretches, buried 'neath the stones;
Or raging yet, with torments from the fire;
With matchless wickedness, he strikes his lyre.[aa]
'Tis said in ecstacy of thought he viewed
That new and famed metropolis that should
In beauty and magnificence, efface
All former efforts of the human race:
And to a crowded people, should impart
Comfort and health,—the true design of art.
Though of his species he had been the bane,
Succeeding ages ever should maintain
That Nero Claudius Cæsar had not lived in vain.

Now a presiding demon he appears,
Glorying over ruin,—'midst the cheers
Of crowding parasites, replete with joy
He sings aloud the fall of ancient Troy :
Old Priam's death, proud Hecuba's sad fate,
And all the ills, the wily Greeks create ;
The famous wooden horse—the carnage dire
And now analogous—the murderous fire ;
How 'scaped the son, Rome's great progenitor,
How from the flames, his aged sire he bore :—

But Maro told that tale ; my humble lay,
Though it resemble but the feeble ray
Of midnight taper to the noonday sun
When matched with his : still shall it onward run,
In gratitude to Thee, Almighty Power,
Who in immensity of space doth tower,
Boundless and eternal ; yet can descry
Minutest objects in this hither sky ;
Still let thy blessings on this land descend ;
From every ill our country still defend :
And on our widow'd Queen Thy bounties shed.
Let guardian angels hover round her head ;
Inspire her mind with wisdom, to subdue
The feuds of jarring factions ; and imbue
Her heart with true religion, virtue, grace,
In love of Thee, to emulate her race :

To do Thy will, to govern in Thy name,
The good of all—let be her constant aim ;
That the whole nation, with one voice may pray,
God shorten not Victoria's reign a day !

END OF THE FIRST BOOK.

NOTES TO BOOK I.

ᵃ Page 9. The murder of Agrippina and Octavia, the mother and wife of Nero, as related in *Tacitus' Annals*, Book xiv.

ᵇ Page 9. Suetonius' *Life of Nero*, sect. 38.

ᶜ Page 10. This description of the old City is attested by Tacitus, Livy, and other ancient writers, thereby contradicting the saying that Augustus found it of bricks and left it of marble.

ᵈ Page 11. Suetonius' *Life of Nero*, sect. 38.

ᵉ Page 11. *Tacitus' Annals.* Book xx., sect. 38.

ᶠ Page 12. Nero's passion for music is related by all ancient historians.

ᵍ Page 13. "And Paul dwelt two whole years in his own hired house, and received all that came in unto him; preaching the Kingdom of God, and teaching those things which concern the Lord Jesus Christ, with all confidence, no man forbidding him."—Acts xxviii., v. 30, 31.

ʰ Page 13. Pliny's letter to Trajan, in which he says the Christians were wont to meet together before it was light, and to sing a hymn to Christ.

ⁱ Page 15. The Author has taken a liberty here, as the Isle of Cyprus was not a Proconsular government; Sergius Paulus was Governor under the title of Deputy.—Acts xiii. 7.

ʲ Page 15. Valerius Asiaticus, put to death in the 7th year of the reign of Claudius, as related by Tacitus : *Annals*, Book xi., sect. 1—3. For adopting the son, the Author has no authority except that the orphan family were received into the Emperor's household; brought up by him, and educated under his direction.

ᵏ Page 16. Dionysius the Areopagite, converted to Christianity by St. Paul at Athens.—Acts xvii. 34.

ˡ Page 16. "Luke, the beloved physician."—Coloss. xv. 14.

ᵐ Page 16. "But Paul was suffered to dwell by himself, with a soldier that kept him."—Acts xxviii. 16. To whom he was chained at considerable length, according to the Roman custom, by his right hand to the left of the soldier.

^o Page 16. "Only Luke is with me."—2 Tim. iv. 11.

^o Page 17. "Because that for the hope of Israel I am *bound with this chain*."—Acts xxviii. 20. "The Lord give mercy unto the house of Onesiphorus, for he oft refreshed me and was not *ashamed of my chain*."—2 Tim. i. 16. Also St. Paul's Epistle to Philemon, where he speaks of his bonds.

^p Page 17. Postscript to 2 Tim.; when Paul was brought before Nero the second time.

^q Page 17. "And all that sat in the council, looking steadfastly on him, saw his face as it had been the face of an Angel."—Acts vi. 15.

^r Page 18. For this and other facts of Paul's speech, see 2 Tim. iv.

^s Page 18. "And I was delivered out of the mouth of the lion."—2 Tim. iv. 17. This may be interpreted literally, or as Lardner and other commentators understand it, that by the lion the Apostle means Nero.

^t Page 19. Suetonius' *Life of Nero*, sect. 38.

^u Page 20. *Tacitus' Annals*, Bk. xv. sect. 38.

^v Page 21. "All the Saints salute you, chiefly them that are of Cæsar's household."—Phill. iv. 22.

^w Page 22. It is recorded that a dark cloud was seen to hover over Mount Vesuvius several days previous to its destructive eruption, when the cities of Pompeii and Herculaneum were destroyed, and the elder Pliny lost his life; and though this happened some few years after the fire of Rome, that is in the reign of Titus, still the Author thinks he has not exceeded the license generally allowed to poems of this description in introducing it.

^x Page 23. *Tacitus' Annals*, Bk. xv. sect. 38.

^y Page 24. *Tacitus' Annals*, Bk. xv. sect. 41.

^z Page 24. The reader will see this in Ovid, and the Author was led to the comparison by witnessing the fire of St. Peter's Church, Belgrave Square.

^{aa} Page 26. Suetonius' *Life of Nero*, sect. 38.

BOOK II.

PAUL AT ATHENS;

OR,

THE CONVERSION OF DIONYSIUS.

ARGUMENT.

The desolation of Rome after the conflagration compared to the demolition of an ant hill. Nero strongly suspected of having been the author of the fire—Great tumult in Rome—Reaches Antium, where he had resolved on charging the crime to the Christians—Calls Epaphroditus his Freedman to summon the Senate, and Paul as the leader of the Christians to be brought before them — Epaphroditus, his meditations in his walk through the ruins of the City to the Palace of Sergius Paulus situated beyond the Tiber—Great grief in his household to divert which Dionysius relates his conversion at Athens —The court of the Areopagus—Its nature and office—Paul exciting the people by his preaching is brought before them—Dionysius one of the judges—The appearance of the court by night—Paul is accused of blasphemy—Makes his defence—Favourably heard till he speaks of the Resurrection when he is ridiculed and dismissed—The court dissolves, and Dionysius contemplates alone the nature of Paul's doctrine—Contrasts it with the philosophy of the Heathens—Resolves to seek Paul—Is overtaken by him—And appoints a time to meet him at his own house—Dionysius' reflections—Assembles his household who in silence await the coming of Paul—He arrives and commences his discourse—In anticipation of Dionysius requiring a miracle quotes the prophecies from the Hebrew books and preaches Jesus—Dionysius convinced asks to be baptized—Epaphroditus enters and acquaints them all with Nero's decree.

THE CONVERSION OF DIONYSIUS.

Who has not seen when pacing o'er the meads,
How every small surrounding object pleads
Infinite wisdom in great Nature's God ?
E'en in the simple animated clod,
Where the industrious ant in myriads dwell,
Serving a nation for a citadel :
Who has not witnessed how that insect tribe,
The arts, the workings of our kind describe ;
And felt how good, how provident in this,
As in his greater works our Maker is ?
In all, to all, o'er Earth's and Air's extreme,
Omniscient, omnipresent, and supreme.
Who has not marked when that the plough has riven,
Their little world, they in confusion driven,
Are with calamity unlooked for scared ?
Then if small things with great may be compared,
Such was the consternation that o'ercome,
Dismayed, dismantled, desolated Rome.

Now through assembled crowds loud murmurs ran,
Whence the disaster,—whence the fire began,—

Who first discovered,—who first gave alarm,—
All asked each other,—but the tyrant's arm,
The threats of Nero's freedmen in their ears,
Sunk all their hearts in base unmanly fears;
At length some spirit bolder than the rest,
Ventured a whisper; though but half expressed,
It whispering spread,—then others louder spoke,
Till from the whole community it broke,
That Nero's men with torches had been seen,[a]
That he himself to gratify his spleen,
And gain renown infernal, had been known,
Though in disguise to lead his creatures on;
Pointing, directing, urging all their ire,
When from the Circus first appeared the fire.

As in the torrid zone on Afric's coast,
For gold and ivory famed, but for that most
Which sullies human nature; causing man
For sordid love of lucre to trepan
And bind his fellow creature,—branding all,
With curses deeper than aught since the Fall:
Far as the eye can reach, a small white speck,
By skilful seaman on the slaver's deck,
Is seen, is watched, until it fill the sky,—
Teeming with vengeance as the cloud draws nigh,
A low deep hollow murmur o'er the main
Steals on the ear—then thunder, lightning, rain,
Bursts on the vessel's side—a hurricane.

So from a simple whisper there arose
Tumult and uproar, threatening the repose
Of all within,—for vengeance calling loud,
The people now form one impetuous crowd :
Soon to a pitch of fury it attained,
And Antium[b] reached, where Nero had remained,
In secret conclave; plotting—giving birth
To further crimes, whose fame should fill the earth.

Roused by the danger of the threatening storm,
To hide his machinations by the form
Of law—he to Epaphroditus[c] calls :—
" Issue my edict that within the walls
" Of Rome's great Capitol,[d] the Senate meet,
" At the third hour o'the morn,—send to greet
" The Captain of the Guard ; bid him produce
" His prisoner Paul ; 'tis time we did reduce
" The growing evil of this baneful sect :
" In our high office as the Pontifect
" We'll make due supplication to the Gods ;
" Assemble all the Lictors with their rods,
" To attend me to the Capitol—away !"
The Freedman turned, accustomed to obey.

With sad and sinking heart foreboding ill,
He hastes to Rome to do the Emperor's will ;
Sought out the Œdiles, bade them all prepare
A sacred lustrum—Cæsar would be there—
Dispatched a slave to Tigellinus[e] strait,
To those whose duty 'twas to promulgate

The decree, he gave—then when parting day
Shed its mild lustre o'er his blackened way,
Where nought but desolation met his eye,
Contrasting strangely with the azure sky,
Illumined now with bright successive hues,
All peering, changing, lessening, till they lose
Their beauty in grey twilight—index this,
To all we fancy of eternal bliss ;
Majestic emblem of creative might !
That the sad work of man's destructive spite:—
He musing walked to where old Tiber's flood
Seemed to divide the evil from the good :
With unscathed palaces the one side bright,
The other blacker than the coming night,
A melancholy sad unseemly sight ! [f]

He crossed the bridge where legions had of yore,
In conflict met and dyed the stream with gore ;
Then stopt to ruminate on days of old,
When foreign foes, ambition, faction, gold
Had brought the city to destruction's verge,
And wars on wars had been the people's scourge :
But ne'er till now had Rome received a blow,
Wanton barbarity only could bestow ;
Not Marius, Sylla, Catiline, had vowed
(Whose names with fame infernal are endowed)
Such dark, ferocious vengeance on mankind,
As he had witnessed filled the tyrant's mind ;
Their evil thoughts, though born and reared in strife,
Nurtured in crime—with blood and slaughter rife,—

Dared never contemplate so foul a deed,
As that presented to a monster's need.
With mournful aspect he approached the gate,
Where Sergius Paulus* dwelt in noble state,
Anxious to learn—more anxious to impart,
The sad forebodings of his troubled heart;
For he was one of Nero's household, who
Had followed Paul, his doctrines round to strew;
And spread through heathen cities as he went,
When on some secret mission he was sent.

Within that mansion sorrow held her seat:
The Christian lord desirous to entreat
With courtesy and love the friends of Paul,—
(Paulina^h too, in bitterness of gall)—
He sought their presence, knowing that in grief
Communion and condolence give relief.
Thoughtful and sad, Valerius^i was there
Watching with earnest gaze the drooping fair,
Who, with dishevell'd locks and tearful eyes,
Could not the anguish of her soul disguise;
The piteous look, the involuntary sob,
Would e'en the goddess Melancholy rob
Of all her woe—but o'er her pensive brow
A placid resignation mantles now:
He had not openly her creed embraced—
The mystic cross had not his frontlet graced;
But to her sire and all his house 'twas known,
The faith of her he loved he made his own;

Since that dread night, when consternation seized
On all around : reflection had not eased
His troubled mind ; to visit Paul again,
Or some devoted follower of his train,
The fire forbade.   Now seated by his side,
The learned Dionysius[j] was his guide ;
Him to instruct and gratify all hearts,
His own conversion he with grace imparts ;
With marked attention every ear was bowed,
As this exalted Christian spake aloud :—

    " When Paul first came to Athens, I was then
" Of that illustrious school, a denizen ;
" For at that font of learning I had sipt ;
" In Egypt's mysteries had fondly dipt :
" In time to Areopagus I rose
" A special dignity, reserved for those
" Whose deeds the Senate's sanction can obtain—
" Whose maxims challenge Virtue's loftiest strain ;
" A grave assembly,—men of every sect,
" The love of truth and wisdom can collect ;—
" A judgment-seat no power can contravene—
" The first tribunal Greece or Rome has seen ;—
" Where rulers, sages, senators, combine,
" Justice administer, and the laws define ;
" Award due honors to the wise and great ;
" Of evil doers purify the state ;
" Condemn for murder, treason, blasphemy,
" Hear all appeals, and set the guiltless free.[k]

" Followed by crowds they found him setting forth
" Some other gods, before unknown on earth :
" His urgent manner, his impressive tongue,
" Incite the multitude, both old and young ;
" Idle, inquisitive, prone to hear and tell
" Whatever from the lips of strangers fell ;
" They gather round, and fain would know the cause,
" Why he despised and set at nought their laws ;
" For daily in the market he denounced
" Our idle worship, and his own pronounced
" Worthy of God alone to entertain ;
" Or even Man with reason to sustain.

" At eve the people brought him to our court,
" Where some through envy, some through ill report,
" Would know what 'twas this babbler had to say,
" For so they termed this marvel of the day ;
" Why with such earnestness he swept away
" Time-honor'd oracles, and made display
" Of doctrines new,—treating with laughter, scorn,
" The Gods, whose temples numberless adorn
" Our sacred city,—famed in times gone by,
" For warlike deeds and proud philosophy.

" On that same hill where rode the god of war,
" In terrors clad, triumphant in his car ;
" As our progenitors had fabled erst,
" 'Mongst other dæmons now for e'er accursed ;
" Where Socrates,[1] the offspring and the light
" Of heathen wisdom, and of learning bright,

" Stood in his native innocence arrayed,
" The blank injustice of his fate pourtrayed—
" Whose condemnation is the blood-stained spot,
" On Athens' annals time will never blot ;
" With heathen fortitude poured forth his soul.
" When drinking to its dregs the poisoned bowl :
" Was Paul arraigned.   I sat in judgment there,
" With thirty more his sentence to declare ;
" But first to give him audience and decide
" What to condemn, what doctrines to deride :
" For some had charged him as a wandering Jew
" Intent on strife ; while other, nobler few,
" Contended for his right, whate'er his sect,
" His creed to publish, other gods erect ;
" Where Stoics, Epicureans, both desire
" To hear the man, who, though in mean attire,—
" In foreign accent and imperfect speech
" Astounding all that stood within his reach—
" Would by his energy and language bold,
" Subvert our gods of ivory and gold ;
" And from his own philosophy propound
" A purer worship, not in Athens found.

" The sun in golden majesty had sunk,
" And his last lingering rays had shrunk
" Before the lustre of that spangled sky,
" Leaving the heavens a cloudless canopy :
" The silvery moon hangs like a sacred lamp
" With due solemnity our course to stamp ;
" On the Piræus glancing down her beams
" And o'er the dimpling waves translucent gleams ;

" Casting a pale and melancholy light,
" On the Acropolis, and the lofty site
" Of Pallas' temple, whose porticoes look down
" In darkening shadows, and portentous frown ;
" As if the voice that issued from that gloom,
" Her altars threatened and foretold her doom.

" Erect, serene, on the delinquent's block,[m]
" Facing his judges, Paul withstood the shock
" Of his assailants, who from the accuser's stone,
" With vile aspersions, in malicious tone,
" Charged him with blasphemy, treason to the state,
" And lesser crimes I need not here relate :
" Firmly resolved his doctrine to maintain,—
" His mission to fulfil,—Paul, in a vein
" Of fervid eloquence, and just rebuke,
" So well recorded by our brother Luke ;
" Reproves us all for superstitious rites,
" Then in persuasive, earnest, mood invites
" Our supplications to the 'Unknown God,'
" Whose fane he saw, as Athens' streets he trod :
" Him he proclaimed the One we long had sought ;
" He was the God whose worship now he taught ;
" His God and ours,—the Holy, Just and True,
" Whose pure existence was revealed to few :
" Who dwells on high, in Ether's boundless space,
" And not to Man beholden for a place,
" Wherein to fix His attributes, or trace
" With cunning exquisite, His Holy face ;
" Whose temple is the Universe, whose shrine
" The human mind, reflecting the Divine :

" As yon pale moon reflects the sun's strong light,
" Faint emblem of his glory—not his might ;
" Who caused, created, governs all on earth,
" In whom we live, and move and have our birth.

   " In such a strain, with reasoning, so acute,
" That not the wisest ventured to refute,
" He wins our favour ;—lifting up his voice,
" That seemed to make the very hill rejoice,
" He then declared—' This God has summoned all,
" ' In every clime, and nation to recall,
" ' Repent their sins ; at once to seek His name,
" ' Whom He has sent their errors to reclaim ;
" ' And has forenamed a fixed, a final day,
" ' When they shall put aside this mortal clay,—
" ' Shall stand in resurrection from the bier,
" ' Before His throne their lasting doom to hear :
" ' To prove His might, God raised him from the dead,
" ' To found that Gospel I am called to spread.'n

   " Such strange disclosure, such unheard-of tale,
" Provoked the more to scoff, some few to rail :
" E'en in the court, the sneer, the sapient smile,
" Sarcastic glances, intimate the while,
" Though they could not condemn, they must deride
" What human reason, Nature's laws denied :
" Therefore he might depart, and when disposed,
" They'd hear again the doctrine he proposed :
" Then they dismissed him, but some few there were,
" Who whispered Paul, and bade him not despair.

" While he with holy confidence inspired,
" Unmindful of their gibes, unscathed retired,
" The court dissolved: and 'ere their homes they gained,
" Of that assemblage I alone remained.
" The noisy hum of men had died away,
" And solemn silence had resumed her sway ;
" No wind disturbed the waters of the deep,
" That round our noted promontory sweep :
" The night was tranquil as an infant's sleep :
" In heavenly contemplation I recalled,
" Once and again, the words that had appalled
" Mine inmost soul : the sophists called divine,
" To search for truth our energies incline,
" Assuage our passions, all their rules combine,
" To make men noble, virtuous, wise and just :
" But whence the Spirit ? where the hand that must
" Direct, control our being, and pervade
" The image of Himself, but He that made ?
" Where the submission to Creation's God ?
" What homage paid to His all-ruling rod ?

" Philosophy is mortal, and can soar
" No higher than the Earth, can dream no more
" What our immortal future state absorbs,
" Than what exists in those celestial orbs,
" That now illuminate the spanless sky :
" How shall such rules with heavenly wisdom vie !
" Pythagoras and Plato but descried
" The soul's immortal essence ; Paul supplied
" A proof of its existence, and made known
" The wondrous means by which to him 'twas shewn.

" 'Time had not yet the mystery revealed,
" For some great cause from them it was concealed :
" Thus while the Samian laboured in the dark,
" Paul was ignited by the vital spark
" Of fire from heaven ;—not as our poets hold, °
" Of heathen tales, in verse harmonious told :
" But with the torch of truth, to light mankind,
" The soul's immortal destiny to find ;
" Made manifest by One, whom Paul affirmed,
" Had by his death the grace divine confirmed ;
" One, who united in his short-lived span,
" The excellence of God with perfect Man.

  " Can such things be— the dead to rise again—
" Immortal things to mortal flesh pertain ?
" How could I solve such mystery profound,
" Where Nature's laws, seem'd severed or unbound ?
" Thus reasoning with myself, I called to mind,
" That for hereafter Man had always pined :
" In Egypt, Asia, ev'n in Greece and Rome, ᵖ
" Their mysteries taught, their votaries sought a home
" Beyond the skies ; on some far distant shore
" Where never mortal man had breathed before—
" Where warfare, toil, and sorrows were to cease,
" For e'er to dwell in harmony and peace ;
" Without a guide but legendary lore,
" With fabled gods and heroes scribbled o'er.
" In all my meditations, I had thought
" Such mode, with fraud and fallacy was fraught ;
" Had sifted every doctrine from my youth,
" In all to seek, in none to find, the truth ;

" Therefore I weighed the more what Paul averred,
" Though he the court's derision had incurred :
" While doubts on doubts my beating heart oppressed,
" And my perturbed mind could find no rest,
" Like the returning dove to Noah's hand,
" Weary with soaring, fruitless for the land ;
" Some monitor,—some spirit seem'd to say :
" ' Search for thyself, and be not led astray
" ' By that philosophy which only shews
" ' How little Man can add to what he knows ;
" ' Shall He who made the Universe compare
" ' With Man, whose utmost knowledge is a snare,
" ' To forge and fashion systems to his mind—
" ' To train, subdue, and keep in bonds his kind ?
" ' Seek then for Paul, and learn from him the way
" ' To turn thy present darkness into day.'

" Not disobedient to the warning voice,
" That though it spake not gave me not a choice,
" I left the hill, the *agora* ⁹ had crossed,
" My thoughts on that night's incident engrossed,
" When sounds of footsteps following in my track,
" Arrest my lucubrations ;—looking back,
" Ere I could speak, a figure cried aloud :—
" ' Dion—where now—why leavest thou the crowd ?'
" Then drawing near, ' Thou seekest Paul, dost not?'
" I gave assent,—" Behold him on the spot—
" ' I know thy wants ; to-morrow at thy home,
" ' Assemble all thy household,—I will come
" ' At the third hour, and then we will discourse
" ' On what my heaven-taught spirit would enforce ;

" ' And He who knows all hearts, prepare thine own,
" ' To quit the errors under which 't has grown ;
" ' Dispose thy mind his Gospel to receive,
" ' That thou and thine may worship and believe :
" ' Till then farewell ; of night what hours remain.
" ' Ponder my words,—all other thoughts restrain.'

 " My heart's desire so soon accomplished, I
" Hastened my steps, determined to apply
" Alone my utmost faculties to sift
" What seemed to me, beyond a mortal's gift :
" To know my thoughts—anticipate my wish !—
" Such evil spirit as the son of Kish,*
" Whom I had read of in the Hebrew scroll,*
" Inquired of erst— must have possessed his soul :
" To what could be attributed his art,
" What god, what dæmon, did their aid impart ?
" If not the force of magic, it must be
" Some great, some superhuman agency.
" Inclined our ancient worship to discard,
" With favour Paul's new doctrine to regard,
" I reached my home, and musing on the past,
" I felt as if an eye were on me cast,
" That searched my failing heart, where lay concealed,
" Some gathering doubts, that would not let me yield
" Implicit credence to his marvellous tale ;
" Scruples and doubts at every turn assail
" My half-according spirit, till at length
" The time appointed called for all my strength,
" ' To meet his disquisitions, and to ask
" Some deed decisive to complete his task.'

" Our morn's repast soon ended, at my call,
" My wife Damaris" and her maidens all,
" Together with my slaves and freedman stand,
" With those who sought instruction at my hand,
" To witness his reception, and to see
" What manner o' man this stranger Paul might be :
" For they had heard of the commotion made
" In Athens' streets, and their account had laid
" To hear this same new doctrine, from the tongue
" Of one whose powerful eloquence had wrung
" Unwilling testimony from sages grave,
" Whose solemn judgment he alone would brave.

" Still as the groves when scarce a sound is heard,
" From buzzing insect, or from warbling bird ;
" When summer zephyrs stir not leaf or herb,
" The sophist's meditations to disturb :
" A noonday solitude that serves to curb
" Their lighter thoughts :—so now impressed with awe,
" All other objects from our minds withdraw ;
" When Paul appeared, and uttering aloud
" A benediction, thus his cause avowed.

" ' Moved by the Spirit, I am come to thee,
" ' O Dion ! famed for thy philosophy,
" ' To offer to thy soul Salvation's gift ;
" ' From out a world of disputation lift
" ' Thine o'ercharged mind,—thy sophisms to impeach,—
" ' Instruct thee how the ways of truth to reach :

" ' To help thee our new doctrine to embrace,
" ' It's birth divine to set before thy face;
" ' To speed thee on in this immortal race.
" ' Wouldst thou enquire still further of our creed?
" ' Of stronger witness dost thou stand in need?
" ' What yesternight I spake before the court,
" ' Thou'dst have me now by some strange act support?
" ' I know thine heart—thy motive can descry,
" ' And am content thy wish to gratify:
" ' Give ear then to my speech, while I unfold
" ' A miracle, thy senses may behold.

" ' 'The men inspired who wrote this holy book,'
" (From underneath his robe the scroll he took,)
" ' From first to last have prophesied of one,
" ' Who at this time his earthly course should run:
" ' From Moses, he who first described the flood,
" ' Whom your own poets partly understood,'
" ' Whose words and deeds are emblems, types of those
" ' Revealed secrets, which at once disclose
" ' The goodness, mercy, wisdom, power divine,
" ' That with our sacred mysteries entwine:—
" ' To all the other prophets, who foretold,
" ' In language plain, intelligent and bold,
" ' The nature of Christ's kingdom, and his birth,
" ' The time, the place, his sojourn here on earth,
" ' His sorrows, sufferings, cruel death they state—
" ' E'en the minutest circumstance relate:
" ' All, in succession, labour to fulfil,"
" ' In Jesus' person, what their words instil.

" ' And is not this a miracle?   What more
" ' Can'st thou desire?   For centuries before
" ' Some great event, that human tongue should dwell
" ' On its vast import, and its means foretell!
" ' Thou thinkst it strange that God should raise the dead,
" ' And is't not strange that Man should thus be led
" ' To the foreknowledge of his Maker's will;
" ' On future generations to distill
" ' His sacred promise; and for Man to see
" ' In every act accomplish'd His decree?
" ' Not this alone, but Gentile nations round,
" ' In our prophetic books their fate have found:
" ' Assyria, Persia, Macedonia's fall,
" ' The truth of our predictions must recall; '
" ' All this thou knowest, our volume it has passed
" ' Into your language—with your works are classed.' '

   " ' Then from Esaias, whom before he named,
" He read aloud, and when compared, exclaimed:—
" ' This Jesus whom I preach, is He they slew;
" ' The mute, the slaughtered Lamb—by that vile crew
" ' Despised, rejected, but to those made known,
" ' By signs and wonders, whom He calls his own;
" ' Who now like me, to distant regions bear
" ' His hallowed name, His saving grace declare;
" ' And every point the prophet entertained,
" ' Are now by living witnesses maintained:
" ' Already for their faith, some few have died,
" ' Shedding their blood for Jesus crucified;
" ' While persecution others' strength have tried,
" ' By scourgings, stripes, His name have glorified:

" Reckon'd as nought when put into the scale
" With gifts, rewards, His followers never fail."

" When on these wonders he began to touch,
" His clear impassioned eloquence was such
" As soon to bring conviction to our hearts :
" To me his faith he once for all imparts,
" And, kneeling, I implored he would baptize
" Me and my household,—first he bade me rise—
" ' Kneel not to me !   I also am a man,'
" He frowning said ; ' but tell me if you can
" ' Dost thou—do these—believe what I have taught ?
" ' Think not by sophistry your minds are caught :
" ' But search and judge yourselves, and tell me then
" ' If our Messiah come within the ken
" ' Of that sublime description I have read ;
" ' Dost thou believe, and Dion wilt thou tread
" ' In that same path his Gentile followers do ?
" ' Acknowledge Him to be the Saviour true—
" ' The only Mediator 'twixt God and man—
" ' The self atonement that removes the ban—
" ' The curse of sin by Satan introduced ;
" ' When from their faith our parents he seduced ?'

" I, answering, said : ' Paul, thou hast reasoned
        right,
" ' Hast on my darkened soul let in the light :
" ' Hast shewn to me philosophy, how vain !
" ' When first the knowledge of the truth we gain :

E

" ' I do believe that Jesus is the Son
" ' Of our Almighty Ruler, and the One
" ' To whom all power on Earth, in Heaven is given ;
" ' Who from my heart all other gods has driven ;
" ' Receive us then within His holy gate,
" ' That for our sins He may propitiate.'

    " ' Dion,' he said ; ' because thou hast had proof,
" ' Thou wilt no longer hold thyself aloof ;
" ' Those words indelible, that Jesus spake
" ' To him who toils and suffers for His sake
" ' In distant Ind, reflecting from afar,
" ' 'Mongst nations sunk in ignorance, the Star
" ' Of Bethlehem,—thy spirit can conceive :
" ' Blessed are those who see not, yet believe.[aa]
" ' Nathless I gladly offer thee and thine,
" ' As the first-fruits of Athens, at the shrine
" ' Of His new Temple, finished without hands ;
" ' Admit thee in the Holy Gospel's bands :
" ' As Philip did Candace's Eunuch find,
" ' Willing in spirit, of inquiring mind,
" ' And did thereon baptize him in the faith,
" ' So will I thee, regardless of the scathe,
" ' From earthly powers or rulers I may reap,
" ' And charge thee stedfast in that faith to keep :'
" With that he calls for water—but I hear
" A stranger in the vestibule.   Draw near,
" Epaphroditus !"—he it was who came
And whom now Sergius Paulus called by name :

" Welcome our brother Christian, draw near and say
" What brings thee here ? what tidings sad I pray—
" What new communication clouds thy brow ?
" Welcome thou art, but some dire hap I trow
" Has brought thee to my dwelling—What of Paul ?
" Take courage, friend, and speak—Are we not all
" Bound in one holy bond, prepared to fly
" To his assistance, for his cause to die ?"
" Alas !" the Freedman said, " thine aid is vain
" For Paul will ne'er his liberty regain ;
" His doom is fixed—once more, and 'tis the last—
" To-morrow's morn,"—a bitter sigh here passed
Paulina's lips—" Oh, say not so !" she cried,
" On me, on me,—let Cæsar's wrath be plied ;
" I was the cause, 'twas I who took him where—"
" Nay, daughter, nay, 'twas God who sent him there,
" And thou wert but His instrument—beware
" Lest that thy o'erwrought feelings may prevent,
" The succour Luke so recently has lent :"
So spake the sire, while Nero's man stood near,
With quivering lip—first staunched the starting tear,
Then in a mournful hesitating tone,
His master's vengeful, vile, decree made known.

At his recital each one stood aghast—
With dark presages all were overcast ;
In bitter anguish Sergius' bosom burned,
As on Paulina every eye was turned ;
How beat her heart in apprehension's throe !
Who shall recount the measure of her woe ?

For father, brethren, lover, friends she grieved ;
But, above all, for him who had achieved
The triumph of the Gospel in their hearts :
In fitful sighs and agony she starts,—
Till resignation overcoming all,
She breathes to Heaven a fervent prayer for Paul.[bb]

END OF THE SECOND BOOK.

---

^a Page 33.   Suetonius' *Life of Nero*, section 38.

^b Page 34.   The birth-place of Nero, and a palace; his country residence, about six miles from Rome.

^c Page 34.   The freedman and Secretary of Nero, according to Tacitus; whether it be the same Epaphroditus mentioned by St. Paul in his Epistle to the Philippians has never I believe been determined; —but the fact of the Apostle's imprisonment at Rome, and the assistance he had received from this Epaphroditus, so remarkably expressed in the 25th verse of the 11th chapter, "and he ministered to my wants,"—who from his office would have the power and the means of doing so, as well as of alleviating his sufferings—together with his earnest recommendation, chapter xi. verse 26 to the end, and concluding his letter with the salutation of "those who are of Cæsar's household"—a salutation not mentioned in any other of his Epistles— and finally his trusting him with the Epistle—when combined, afford strong internal, or presumptive evidence sufficient to warrant the author in adopting him as one and the same person.

^d Page 34.   The Temple of Jupiter Capitolinus escaped the great conflagration, but was afterwards destroyed by fire in the reign of Vespasian.

^e Page 34.   Sofonius Tigellinus, the Captain of the Guard, who had charge of all prisoners sent from the provinces.

^f Page 35.   The fire was chiefly confined to the old part of the city, and did not extend beyond the Tiber.

^g Page 36.   Sergius Paulus, Governor or Deputy of Cyprus, was converted to Christianity by Paul and Barnabas on their first visit to that island, A.D. 45.—Acts xiii. 7.

^h Page 36.   Paulina, supposed daughter of Sergius Paulus, not named in history.

ⁱ Page 36.   Valerius, the supposed son of that Valerius Asiaticus

who was put to death through the intrigues of Messalina, but whose family was brought up by Claudius Cæsar.

[j] Page 37. Dionysius the Areopagite, mentioned in Acts xviii. 34, as one of St. Paul's converts at Athens.

[k] Page 37. This account of the nature and office of the Court of Areopagus will be found in accordance with the writings of the ancients.

[l] Page 38. Socrates was condemned to drink poison by this Court about 400 years before the Christian era.

[m] Page 40. The precise spot that formed the area of Mars-hill, where the Court of Areopagus was usually held, has been ascertained by modern tourists; and the two blocks of stone, on one of which St. Paul stood, have been identified.—*St. Paul and his Localities*, by Dr. Aiton, published by A. Hall and Co.

[n] Page 41. The defence that St. Paul made before his judges is taken from the Acts of the Apostles, chapter xvii. verse 19 to the end.

[o] Page 43. Ovid, and many other of the heathen poets and philosophers, have made Promotheus the subject of their pen, therefore must his name and feats have been familiar to all.

[p] Page 43. The desire and sense of a hereafter, though vague and undefinable, seem to have been implanted in the breasts of the ancients of whatever creed or nation.—*Homer*, *Virgil*, &c.

[q] Page 44. The *agora* is synonymous with the *forum* or market place.

[r] Page 45. 1 Samuel xxviii. 7.

[s] Page 45. The whole of the Hebrew Books were translated into the Greek language under the immediate direction of Ptolemy Philadelphus, king of Egypt, about 260 years before the Christian era, by the labours of seventy eminent Greek scholars (thence called the Septuagint). It is not improbable that a learned heathen philosopher, like our Dionysius, should have been long intimately acquainted with them, more particularly as it is recorded in his Life that he visited Egypt in his youth.—Cave's *Lives of the Fathers*, St. Dionysius, sec. ii.

[t] Page 45. It has been recorded by Baronius, and others who have written on the history of the early Christians, that Dionysius

demanded a miracle from St. Paul before he would consent to become a convert, and that St. Paul restored a blind man to sight to convince him; but the more respectable authorities contend that it was by St. Paul's discourse only he was converted.—Cave's *Lives of the Fathers*, St. Dionysius, sec. iii.

ᵘ Page 46. Damaris was the wife of Dionysius, according to ecclesiastical history; and St. Chrysostom also includes his whole house in the conversion thus effected.

ᵛ Page 47. The whole history of Deucalion contained in the ancient authors is but a reflection of the Mosaic account of the Flood.

ʷ Page 47. It is only necessary to refer the reader to the Books of the Prophets, particularly to the 53rd chapter of Isaiah, for authority for all that is here quoted in St. Paul's discourse with a heathen philosopher; whom it was necessary to convince, by establishing the fact that prophecy fulfilled is in every sense of the word a miracle.

ˣ Page 48. See Isaiah, Jeremiah, Ezekiel, and Daniel; more particularly the latter.

ʸ Page 48. See Note in page 49.

ᶻ Page 49. Acts of the Apostles, x. 26.

ᵃᵃ Page 50. St. Thomas, to whom our Lord addressed these words (St. John's Gospel, xx. 26) devoted himself and his labours to the Indian Peninsula, and finally suffered martyrdom on the coast of Coromandel, according to ecclesiastical history, in the 73rd year of the Christian era.

ᵇᵇ Page 52. If an apology were needed for the introduction of the episode contained in this Book, it should be stated that, upon a careful perusal of the Acts of the Apostles, it would appear that with the exception of Sergius Paulus, Deputy or Proconsul of Cyprus, who was convinced of the truth of St. Paul's preaching by the astounding punishment inflicted on his evil counsellor Elymas, *Dionysius*, the Areopagite, is the only man of rank or learning named by the Holy Evangelist as becoming a convert to that doctrine which the great Apostle of the Gentiles, before all people, and in spite of every hindrance, so unceasingly, so fearlessly, and so zealously advocated. The lives of the immediate successors of the Apostles, and their followers—the Fathers of the Church, as they are termed—have been carefully collected from tradition and the writings of contemporaries, and handed down to us by a Divine of the seventeenth century; and though it may be a pleasing task to trace the propagation of our creed from its infancy, still it is difficult to divest its early growth of that tincture of super-stition and absurdity—that mixture of truth and falsehood, with which the efforts of schismatics, both Greek and Roman, have dis-figured it. In the life of St. Dionysius, it is asserted by some, that he demanded a miracle of St. Paul before he became a con-vert to what at first appeared to him a most improbable tale, and to the belief of which his reason and philosophy presented insuperable objections. That St. Paul might have restored a blind man to sight, and sent him to the philosopher to claim his promise, is possible; but the story rests on too dubious an authority to be readily admitted: and it is equally as possible, and better authenticated, that the Apostle found it more congenial to the spirit of his mission—consequently more conducive to the service and glory of his cause—to overcome so learned a heathen by the force of human reasoning alone, rather than with the aid of superhuman gifts. It is for this therefore that the author has combined the two accounts, and grafted this episode on the inference, that the miracle Dionysius so much desired to witness emanated from the Apostle's own knowledge and experience, on which he would dis-course, and appeal to the understanding of the heathen philosopher, without making a display of those miraculous powers which the poor and ignorant alone would need, and for whom by an all-wise and bene-ficent Providence they were, it seems, more particularly designed.

" To the Poor the Gospel is preached."—*St. Luke* vii., v. 22.

BOOK III.

—

PAUL BEFORE NERO;

OR, THE

TRIAL AND CONDEMNATION OF THE CHRISTIANS FOR SETTING FIRE TO THE CITY.

———◆———

ARGUMENT.

Pompey's Temple in the Capitol; one of the few buildings which had escaped the general conflagration, and which had been closed ever since the death of Julius Cæsar, is opened by order of the Emperor for the trial of St. Paul—The Senate assemble—Nero ascends to the Capitol amidst the sound of trumpets, and the execration of the people, attended by Seneca, Tigellinus, the Consuls and Lictors, followed by Paul, and surrounded by his guards—He takes his seat and addresses the Senate; commands Paul to be brought forward, and publicly accuses him of setting fire to the city—The surprise of the Senate—Paul's defence—Nero's reply—Calls his witnesses, Phygellus and Hermogenes—Paul's reproof—Alexander the coppersmith interrupted by Nero, who calls on Gallio for explanation—The Coppersmith's evidence continued—The horror of the Senate at his recital—His evidence concluded and confirmed—Sergius Paulus speaks in his defence—Abruptly stopped by Nero—The Senate decide against Paul—Nero passes sentence, and condemns Paul to be thrown to wild beasts—Paul claims the privilege of a Roman—Nero's rage—Seneca interferes, and endeavours to assuage him and persuade Paul to obtain pardon—Paul's indignant reply—Nero consigns Paul to a dungeon, and dismisses the assembly.

THE TRIAL AND

CONDEMNATION OF THE CHRISTIANS

FOR SETTING FIRE TO THE CITY.

———•———

THE morn arrived—the Conscript Fathers met,
Where the first Cæsar paid ambition's debt ;
Where Brutus' dagger gained immortal fame,
And Cassius added lustre to his name ;
Where lay the master-spirit of the age,
The hero, poet,[a] orator and sage,—
The greatest man that mortal e'er shall see—
Fit sacrifice to Rome and liberty.
More than a century had passed away,
Since Pompey's temple saw the light of day ;[b]
Closed by the Senate when great Julius bled—
By Nero opened, holier blood to shed.
How thronged the Senators around to trace
The ichor still, that stained great Pompey's base ;[c]
As if his rival's heart's best blood had flown,
His and his country's injuries to atone.
How blushed the lost descendants of those men,
Lost to all sense of patriot feeling, when
The man, the cause, for which their fathers slew,
Failed in their hearts such spirit to renew ;

Their minds such great example to admire ;
Or with a spark of freedom to inspire :—
Content a tyrant's edicts to fulfil,
The servile Senate of a monster's will.[d]

Degenerate Rome ! if sons of Rome ye were ;
Where now your boasted liberty, and where
Those sons of freedom, who, for her sake dare,
Risk life and fortune, reputation—share
Their glory with the Commonwealth,—and see
Rome's fame exalted, but when Rome was free ?
Freedom and fame, alas ! together lie,
With Cassius—Brutus 'neath Philippi's sky ;'
Then her renown and ancient glory fled,
But lives to ages in the honoured dead.
Well Brutus spoke in that eventful hour,
When liberty was crushed by tyrant power,
O'er Cassius' bleeding body where he fell,
" Thou last of all the Romans,—Fare thee well !"[f]

The piercing sound of trumpets now announce
The Emperor's approach :—while the crowd denounce
In cries as loud the author of the fire,
He smiles contempt upon their fruitless ire :
Surrounded by his guards, their wrath he knew
Would fall as harmless as the morning dew.
Though against him they rail in bitterest vein,
He had the art their fickle voice to gain ;
Though now their breasts with indignation burn,
He knew they, like the briny tide, would turn ;

And those who now their voices loudest raise,
Would, ere the night, be louder in his praise.

Ascending to the Capitol,* his right
By him supported, who for learning's light—
For virtue and philosophy renowned—
Who once the tyrant for preceptor owned,
Seneca, pride of Rome:*—while on his left
Walked Tigellinus,* of all good bereft;
The Captain of the Guard, since Burrhus died,*
Whose rigid virtues he but ill supplied;
Congenial spirit with the prince he served,
One whose whole life from vice had never swerved.
Then came the Consuls—Lictors with their rods,
Some carrying emblems of their numerous gods;
Last, followed Paul, whose sole attendants were
The man that kept him, and the friend* that dare
Support and consolation tend to one,
Whose trial now his other brethren shun.
Prætorian guards encompassed all the train,
Until the summit of the steps they gain:
Entering the Temple, then the guards dispose
Themselves in stations, while the Senate rose
Their master to receive: whose evil look,
As with a threatening mien his place he took,
Was of some dark intent the certain test:
Terror and awe their slavish minds impressed,
When thus the throng he artfully addressed:—

" Annæus Seneca, Conscript Fathers all,
" I first must to your memory recall,

" How, since the Imperial purple I obtained,
" The Senate's rights have strictly been maintained,'
" The laws enforced, and equal justice done
" Throughout the State ;—from where the rising sun
" Gilds the Caucasian mountains with his beams,
" To Lusitania, where his burnished streams
" Fade in the ocean as he there descends ;
" From East to West where Roman sway extends :
" From North to South, from Caledonia's land
" To utmost Lybia's barren, burning sand ;"
" By nations all, by men of every grade
" Our name is honoured, and our will obeyed."
" I also must recount the licence given
" To all religious sects ;—but one has striven,
" The worship of the gods to controvert,
" Their less than mortal essence to assert.
" Fathers, our reign too merciful has been,
" For the calamity we now have seen ;
" The smouldering ruins that around us lay—
" This dreadful curse that summons us to-day,
" Is the foul deed, the base atrocious crime
" Of Christian miscreants from Judea's clime."
" Nay, start not, Sergius Paulus—we have proof
" Irrefragable :—plead in their behoof
" If that thou think'st the Senate thou canst win ;
" Thy house we hear is tainted with this sin :—
" Of that anon ;—set forth the prisoner Paul :"
The clanging chain re-echoed through the hall,
As with a solemn step and placid mien,
The soldier led him to the space between

Nero and the Senate :—no fear expressed
Or anger there ; but every thought suppressed :
In silence and composure he awaits
The accusation that thus Nero states :—

"Fathers, this aged prisoner you will find
" Chief of that sect all others leave behind
" In their determined hatred to mankind.[p]
" By his own nation scorned, e'en there a pest,
" Our Festus sent him hither to attest
" Something relating to his own vile creed,
" Of which the Jews themselves had taken heed :
" From them to our tribunal he appealed,[q]
" Through our mistaken mercy has concealed,
" Conceived and executed, the foulest crime,
" That e'er was written on the scroll of time :—
" What ! this Imperial city to destroy,
" And all within 't !—no pity, no alloy
" To thy consummate hate ; and to seduce
" Some poor mechanics whom we will produce :[r]
" First, to convert them to thine evil creed,
" Then, to be made partakers in a deed
" Of darkness—death, as if the gods had fled
" The sacred city, whose destinies they led,
" For now eight hundred years, to glory's height,
" All to be sacrificed in one sad night,
" To vile Judeans !—a nation that's despised,
" Famed for all evil, for no virtue prized !
" Our Father Claudius, of illustrious name,
" Seeing their wickedness he could not tame,

" Banished them the city,'—our lenient reign
" Has suffered them within these walls again ;
" And now like harpies hither do they flock
" Our fame to tarnish, and our gods to mock :
" From them has sprung this viler Christian sect,
" Whose bitter malice this man does direct.
" Fathers, the gods are reconciled, and we
" Must now proceed to justice, and to see
" The guilty punished, whosoe'er they be :
" People and Senate, I accuse this man,
" And all belonging to his hateful clan,
" Of firing your city,—deny it if he can !"

   Astounded with the charge the prisoner seems ;
He clasps his hands—his furrowed face, that teems
With tears of woe, is raised to the sky,
As if imploring succour from on high :
The tyrant's object instantly he saw,—
His cause submitted to the Roman law,
Where judges and accusers would combine,
Left him no hope :—to oppose this base design,
He with his wonted energy resolved.
Though dumb the Senators,—their looks evolved
Their different thoughts,—some with insidious eye
Expressive of mistrust and irony,
Averted face, and scarce restrained smile,
Evinced suspicion of the tyrant's guile ;—
Others with face outstretched and lips apart,
And orbs that from their sockets seemed to start,

Gazed upon Paul:—wondering so base a man
Could so provoke the mighty Cæsar's ban;—
Some few dejected, doubting, and distressed,
Their sympathy for the prisoner suppressed:
One seemed alone in meditation lost,
Thoughts of deep worth, his troubled spirit crossed;
But the pressed lip, the fixed yet manly air,
Denote that truth and firm resolve were there.
Solemn the scene, and silent were they all:
That silence broken by the voice of Paul:—

"Cæsar and Senators, if I submit
"To this your jurisdiction, and admit
"The power of your tribunal—'tis because
"I've always taught submission to the laws;
"To induce a reverence for the powers that be,'
"Has been a portion of my ministry.
"Sent a petitioning prisoner to Rome,
"My whole deportment is well known to some
"In office high:—the Captain of the Guard,
"Through whose direction I am kept in ward,
"Can testify this of me, if he will,
"No deeds or words of mine could e'er distil
"Drops of such matchless evil from their hearts,
"Who seek the truth my ministry imparts."
"Truth! what is truth?" cried Nero. "Prisoner, shew!"
"A simple virtue thou canst never know:
"Witness this charge—malicious as absurd,
"Framed to disguise the guilt thou hast incurred;—

" False as thy gods,—to fix on mine and me,
" Thine own deserved and wide-spread obloquy :
" Witness these bonds,—this legionary here,
" Without whose knowledge how could I appear
" Such mighty ills to counsel and direct ?
" No, thy device 'tis easy to detect ;
" From this base charge I hold myself aloof,—
" Deny, defy, and dare thee to the proof."

    " Dost dare me, viper?" Nero said in haste ;
" Soon shalt thou wish those words had been erased
" From out thy memory.—Now will I confute,
" Confound thy foul aspersions—strike thee mute
" With such distinct, decisive evidence,
" As Fathers, shall not leave ye a pretence,
" His guilt to doubt—howe'er it may surprise,
" Or render strange the crime it magnifies.
" First call Phygellus and Hermogenes :"
" Now villain say, what thinkest thou of these ?
" Two of thy late disciples, are they not ?
" Partakers in thy crime—e'en on the spot
" The Circus when ye fired—See, Fathers, see
" If they 're not filled with contrite agony :—
" Not on your heads his vengeance shall he wreak—
" Speak thou, Hermogenes—Phygellus speak,
" And tell the Senate how ye came the dupes
" Of the vile cheats to which the impostor stoops."'

    As our first Parents stood before their God,
Abject, abashed, and trembling at His nod,

When they had broken the Divine command,
And sin and shame and sorrow were at hand;
So stood these two apostates from the truth
By holy Paul converted in their youth;
Now by a monster's artifice cajoled
Their faith to barter for seductive gold;
With downcast looks, and faltering voice, the one,
Speaking for both, to Nero thus begun :—

  " Most mighty Cæsar! Senators, to ye
" We look for succour, and for clemency.
" 'Tis now some twenty years since we became
" Unwilling converts to the Christian name;
" The prisoner making that same name appear,
" A sole sure antidote for evil here,
" Spake of the glories of a life to come,
" And by such arts he lured us from our home,
" Through various troubles brought us here to Rome:
" Now rose our expectation to the sky—
" Then threatened death, eternal misery,
" If with his dictates failed we to comply.
" Worn with privations, destitute and lost,
" We sought a remedy at any cost;
" And when the prisoner pointed to the fire,
" As the best means by which we could acquire
" Support and sustenance,—at once we dived
" Into the gulph his subtlety contrived."

  Though lame and impotent this tale appeared,
The Senators assented, for they feared

The tyrant's wrath :—with increased grief oppressed,
Paul thus the trembling witnesses addressed :—

    " Oh, foolish men! Oh, wretched creatures ! why
" Have ye incurred this lasting infamy ?
" What evil spirit could have caused you twain
" Your Saviour thus to crucify again ?
" What—could ye not resist the tempter's gold ?
" Have ye your souls to sure perdition sold ?
" Your names from out the book of life erased,
" On Satan's list henceforward shall be traced."

    " Cease, prisoner, cease !—denunciations here
" Are vain," cried Nero.—" Fellows, do not fear
" This wretched babbler."—Hither call the smith,
" His evidence shall silence thee forthwith."

    Then, with quick step advancing to the floor,
A figure came whom Paul had seen before
In distant cities ; one who had withstood
His sacred truth and evil gave for good :
His daring front and sinister dark eye,
Proclaimed a heart of hardened villany :
There was a fiendish evil in his look,
That e'en the ardent gaze of Paul could brook ;
A deep, determined, desperate spirit he,
Who came prepared for all emergency.

    Aloud spake Nero:—" Fellow, thou impart
" To us, the Senate, who and whence thou art ;

" Say what thou knowest of the prisoner here,
" And let thy statement be succinct and clear."

   Darting a furtive, fiery glance at Paul,
His tutored tongue these measured words let fall :—
" Thanks, mighty Cæsar—great Augustus, thanks,
" That I have been selected from the ranks
" Of hundred others, ready all to prove
" The prisoner's guilt, and with what arts he strove :
" They call me Alexander,ˣ and I came
" From Ephesus, a place of no mean fame,
" Though mean my occupation ; for I wrought
" E'en as a coppersmith, and much gains I brought,
" Until the evil hour when Paul arrived,
" And to stir up the people he contrived,—
" Telling them a strange mysterious tale
" About one Jesus—trying to prevail
" On all the Jews and Greeks assembled there,
" His God to worship—his belief to share ;
" Denouncing death on all who should refuse
" That name to call on—other gods to choose :—
" 'Twas there I first encountered him, and proved
" To all the people he so much had moved,
" This very Paul had persecuted those—
" Yea, even unto death—who once had chose
" To place their credence on that idle name ;—
" Lighting, by his apostasy, a flame
" That spread through Asia, Macedonia reached,
" At Athens, Corinth, wheresoe'er he preached,
" Threatening the peace of whole communities."—

"Hold, witness, hold!" the artful tyrant cries;
"Say, Junius Gallio,' can this thing be so,
"Proconsul thou, this fellow not to know,
"Nor e'er acquaint the Senate?"   Gallio said,

"I do remember, Cæsar, when I swayed
"The province of Achaia in thy name,
"The prisoner here; and hold me much to blame,
"I did not to the Senate represent
"His power of magic,—for with that he bent
"The minds of people, leading them astray,
"And once at Corinth, causing an affray:
"Brought by the Jews before my judgment seat,
"I found their purpose only was to treat
"Of names and words, and One whom Paul declared
"To be alive,—although his fate was shared
"By other two, who in Tiberius' time
"Were doomed by Pilate in Judea's clime:
"Thinking such controversy would but lead
"To further ill, I bade them not proceed;—
"Dismissed them my tribunal, and inferred
"No future charge 'gainst Paul would be preferred."

"Thou didst not wisely," Nero here replied;
"Thy lenity was wrong:—hadst thou applied
"Summary justice—an example made,
"Our lofty city would not now have laid
"A blackened ruin; nor her blood been spilt,
"To crown the measure of these Christians' guilt;"—

Then turning to the coppersmith, he said,
" Witness, proceed, and be not thou afraid ;
" But state at once the authors of the fire—
" Their means, their schemes, their method we require."

    The Senate's silence not a whisper broke,
As with unaltered look the menial spoke :—
" To seek my craft, O Cæsar! for support
" I came to Rome ; for hither do resort
" Men of all crafts and nations.   Here I found
" My former foe, who, though a prisoner bound,
" Still practised his iniquities, and kept
" His midnight orgies while all others slept.
" Returning from my labour late one night,
" My notice was attracted by a light
" That through an opening gleamed ; I drew near—
" Beheld a scene that thrilled my heart with fear :
" Assembled round a bath of ample size,
" Some twenty men were present to these eyes ;
" Fast in the prisoner's arms a screaming child
" Which, raising to the sky, with gesture wild,
" He muttered an enchantment,—then immersed
" The struggling infant in the bath accursed.
" Heartsick at sight of such inhuman deed,
" I turned away,—but did not far proceed ;—
" For curious yet to know what this could mean,
" I looked again,—and then beheld a scene
" Of greater ill :—all seated round a board,
" Not with refreshing meats or wines well stored,

" But with a plate of flesh—a cup of blood,
" Which I could hear the prisoner, where I stood,
" Pronounce as human—Cæsar, 'tis most true,
" Else may this tongue its speech for ever rue ;—
" Then as each passed a morsel to his mouth,
" The prisoner put to all of them an oath :
" So with the cup, as its contents they sip,
" And stain with human gore each thirsty lip,
" He uttered an anathema 'gainst all,
" Who from that night's resolve should ever fall."

The witness paused :—the fiery meteor's light
Could not create more wonder and affright,
Sweeping the sky with its portentous blaze,
Raising the million's timid, stolid gaze—
Than did this tale the Senator's appal,—
Astonishment and terror fell on all :
Could they believe that such inhuman rites
Had in that place been solemnized for nights !
One shook his head, with doubt and grief distressed,
And would at once the Senate have addressed,—
But Nero stopt him, crying out aloud,
" Sufficient this to satisfy the crowd,
" These murderous miscreants should no longer live ;
" But, witness, thou full testimony give,
" And shew the Senate how thou dost connect
" The city's fall with this pernicious sect."

" Cæsar, next night," the wily fiend resumed,
" Before the burning Circus had illumed

" The sky's extent, again it was my lot
" A flickering flame to spy first near the spot
" Where the previous night I witnessed those
" Revolting revels which mine anger rose :
" Determined now to watch their wicked ends,
" I saw the prisoner and a host of friends
" Issue from out his dwelling, which became,
" From taper's light, a fierce devouring flame :—
" This is, O great Augustus, all I know."

A faint applause the people 'gan to show,
When, at a preconcerted signal given,
A crowd of men to Nero's seat were driven ;
All, all, to testify the tale was true :
Some added further insult, other few
Declared they heard the prisoner Paul invoke
Fire from Heaven, t' annihilate at a stroke
Their sacred temples ; saw his magic power [aa]
Command from hell a fierce and fiery shower,
That should destroy the city at a blow,
And their immortal gods should overthrow.

As the bold chieftain on the frigate's deck,
The ocean's pride—but now, alas, a wreck—
Sees on his lee the inevitable rock,
And with undaunted breast awaits the shock,
That must engulph him and the faithful crew
Who shared his trials, and his triumphs too :
So Paul, with imperturbable, marked brow,
Awaits the sentence that must doom him now,

And all his followers, to some cruel death,
Yet deigns he not to answer e'en a breath :—
When Sergius Paulus, rising from his seat,
Does thus the Senate's sufferance entreat :—

" Illustrious Cæsar, Senators, and men,
" I pray ye hear me :—'Twas the summer when
" Imperial Claudius held the Curule chair,
" And Largus had his Consulate to share :[bb]
" I, Cyprus ruled—at Paphos held my court,
" Where a renowned magician did resort,
" One Elymas by name—whose evil ways
" Had struck the isle with terror and amaze.
" At that same time two men of habits strange—
" Still stranger acts—the country through did range,
" And came to Paphos :[cc] Barnabas the one,
" Who with this Paul their course together run :
" For my award the people did apply,
" Who deeply felt the dæmon's injury ;
" Determined openly their cause to try,
" As in my hall of judgment I was wont,
" I bade those two the sorcerer confront ;
" And never yet was seen the power displayed
" By Barnabas and Paul ; no human aid
" Could give the smitten Elymas relief,
" When blindness covered him with shame and grief ;
" Yea, and with Paul—the look—the word—the deed—
" Were simultaneous ; who then could but read
" The finger there of superhuman might ?"

" Sergius," cried Nero, " thou hast lost thy sight,
" Before a Roman Senate to relate
" Such idle tale this charge to extenuate ;
" What hast thou proved suppose thy tale were true,
" But Paul the greater dæmon of the two ?
" What canst thou say to those infernal rites
" The witness here unwittingly recites ?
" Are not such things sufficient to condemn
" To instant suffering all who practise them ?"

" Believe me, Cæsar," Sergius replied,
" From truth divine, his testimony is wide ;
" Either thy witness wilfully perverts,
" Or an unfounded calumny asserts."

" We'll hear no more—now Senators, decide !
" Guilty, or not ?" the raging monster cried.

The Senate rising, with one voice declared
The prisoner guilty, and all those who shared
His hated creed ;—one universal shout,
That rent the air, from those that were without,
Confirmed the Senate's voice ; when Nero thus
Again addressed the prisoner : " To us
" It now belongs, base wretch, to seal thy fate ;
" And that no further evil to the State,
" From thy misguided followers may accrue,
" Ye all shall perish.   Tigellinus, you
" Search every corner, court, and street in Rome,
" Let not one miscreant escape his doom ;

" Both men and women—all thou find'st confine
" Fast bound and manacled in the Mamertine. ᵈᵈ
" Of this vile creed to stifle every ray—
" Their fate shall make a Roman holiday—
" The time we'll fix, the scene shall be our courts,
" And to it, we will add the Circus' sports :—ᵉᵉ
" Wild beasts from Parthia we will exhibit there ;
" And thou vile hypocrite, shalt be their fare."

   " Nay, nay," cried Paul ; " thy malice I defy—
" A Roman I—a Roman's death I die." ᶠᶠ

   The monster foamed with disappointed rage,
When Seneca stept forth his wrath to assuage.
There was a latent feeling for the sage,
Whose well-stored mind had shewn to him the page
Of earthly wisdom, not of heavenly grace :
A secret awe that crime could not efface :
The one, a silent, seeming deference paid ;
The other, earnestly entreating said :—

   " Thy bounty, Cæsar, when I call to mind— ᵍᵍ
" Thy favour, lifting me above my kind ;
" The wealth and honour so profusely spread
" On this my aged—yet unworthy head,
" Makes me more bold thy notice now to claim ;
" For in thy youthful mind it was my aim
" The wiser rules of government to found,—
" Such rules as to thy glory should redound.

" Of this foul deed, whoe'er the guilty are,
" Thou prove and punish :—but Cæsar, oh! forbear
" To execute thy vengeance on this race.
" Remember, in Tiberius' time, a grace [hh]
" Had passed the Senate, their founder to enrol,
" 'Mong other gods in this famed Capitol :
" In Pilate's acts, his lingering death is writ,"
" Which, with the wonders that attended it,
" He to Tiberius Cæsar did transmit :
" Then let them pass unpunished—for, if true,
" To thee, the greater glory will be due ;
" If false their creed, like Lethe's weed, 'twill rot,
" And in a generation be forgot."

    But too well skill'd in simulation's art,
Nero, impatient, answered with a start :—
" If, Annæus Seneca?—Dost thou say, if?
" Father, thou dost not, canst not know this still—
" This proud, this obstinate, this loathsome race :
" But that no proof be wanting, in the face
" Here of the Senate, and the people too,
" We grant them all free pardon, if they do
" But this vile faith abjure."—To Paul he said,
(A dæmon's smile upon his lip there played)—
" Prisoner, thou'rt free ;—thou mayst redeem thy fate
" If to our gods thou now wilt supplicate." [ii]
With this the sage his friendly prayer must give—
" Call thou on mighty Jupiter and live !—
" Paul, Paul, be wise ; thy followers save and thee :
" Be not the victim of thine obstinacy—
" Accept the proffered pardon and be free."

Paul, on his faith and constancy intent,
To Nero first his ready answer bent :
" Cæsar, I know no other gods but One,—
" To me He was revealed in His Son ;
" To do His will my office is on earth—
" Therefore I count my life of little worth :
" In Him I trust, nor fear what man can do,
" For He 's the only Holy One and true,
" Has power to save, redress, reward, restore ;
" And should He please, to add this blessing more,
" That I and mine for Jesus' sake should die,
" To give us strength His name to glorify."

" Illustrious Roman," to the sage, he said ;
" In all thy pride of wisdom now arrayed :
" Oh ! would that wisdom but the truth receive !
" Could thy philosophy but once perceive
" The difference infinite 'twixt God and man,
" The folly of thy wisdom thou wouldst scan,
" When matched with His—yon insect on the wall,
" Whose powerless instinct serves it but to crawl,
" What thou art to the Almighty is to thee :
" Then seek His truth, thy worldly errors flee.
" The gods thou'dst have me worship are of stone,
" Made by men's hands no better than mine own ;
" My God created me and all mankind.
" Am I then in a stock or stone to find
" Withal to worship ? The God whom I adore
" Dwells in the blue ethereal—lived before

" This world, the sun, the moon, the stars were made,
" From all eternity His power's displayed ;
" In every living thing, throughout all space,
" The great Creator's wisdom I can trace :
" And that inscrutable wisdom did allow
" Mankind to live in ignorance ; but now
" Has sent His Son, His Being to reveal,
" And with His dying blood the truth to seal—
" To lead the way to everlasting life—"

" Enough !" cried Nero, " of this wordy strife ;
" Away with him to the Mamertine.—To thee,
" Sofonius, we give it in charge to see
" New modes of death invented.   Let there be [kk]
" Such mighty show of terror in their fate,
" As from the earth their creed shall extirpate."

" Vain, foolish man !" said Paul as he retired :
" Our creed shall live when nations have expired—
" Increase and flourish—spread from shore to shore,—
" When this thy boasted Empire is no more."

The lictors bound him—hurried him away ;
The Senators' dismissal closed the day.

END OF THE THIRD BOOK.

NOTES TO BOOK III.

^a Page 58. Though none of the productions of this wonderful man have come down to us to authorize the title here given him, few can, or even do, doubt, but his accomplished mind comprehended every degree of literature ; more particularly as his and the succeeding age were ripe with genius and poetry of the highest order.—Virgil, Catullus, Livy, Horace, Ovid, Sallust, &c. &c.

^b Page 58. Suetonius relates in his *Life of Julius Cæsar*, sec. 88, that the Temple of Pompey—being one of the many into which the great Temple of Jupiter in the Capitol was divided—was closed by order of the Senate on his assassination ; the re-opening it on this occasion is an invention of the author's.

^c Page 58. Plutarch's *Life of Julius Cæsar ;* also Shakespeare—

> " E'en at the base of Pompey's statue,
> " Which all the while ran blood, great Cæsar fell."
> *Julius Cæsar,* Act iii., sc. 2.

^d Page 59. To such a degraded state had the Roman Senate arrived at this time, that it was the mere oracle of the Emperor, whose will was law.

^e Page 59. The battle of Philippi was decisive of the liberties of the Commonwealth ; and for awhile the government of so many nations rested chiefly with Octavius Cæsar, (afterwards Augustus), and Mark Antony, till the active and wily ambition of the former proved too much for the indolent and voluptuous lover of Cleopatra, who being defeated by his rival and co-partner in the battle of Actium, the sole power was concentrated in the person of Augustus Cæsar, by the title of Imperator, and so descended to the extinction of the Empire.

^f Page 59. Plutarch's *Life of Marcus Brutus*, also Shakespeare's *Julius Cæsar*, Act v., sc. 3.

^g Page 60. The Capitol was reached by one hundred steps

ascending from the forum or market-place. See Adams's *Roman Antiquities*.

[h] Page 60. Seneca, it is well known, was Nero's tutor. Tacitus' *Annals*, xiii. 2.

[i] Page 60. Sofonius Tigellinus, a creature and parasite of Nero, the companion of all his crimes and debaucheries, made Joint Captain of the Prætorian Guards with Finius Rufus, after the death of Afranius Burrhus.

[j] Page 60. The above-named Afranius Burrhus is supposed to be that Captain of the Guard to whom St. Paul was delivered on his first arrival in Rome, as related in Acts xxviii. 16; and by whose order he was suffered to be at large, through the intercession of the Centurion who had charge of St. Paul on his voyage from Cæsarea to Rome.

[k] Page 60. The person here intended is St. Luke, St. Paul's constant companion during the latter part of his life, if we take the Second Epistle to Timothy to be the last production of the great Apostle to the Gentiles; and which the author humbly thinks its valedictory style fully justifies.

[l] Page 61. See Nero's speech to the Senate at the commencement of his reign.—Tacitus' *Annals*, xiii. 5.

[m] Page 61. For the cardinal boundaries here set to the Roman Empire, see King Agrippa's speech to the Jews.—Josephus' *Wars of the Jews*, ii. 14.

[n] Page 61. That the Roman Empire was then at peace is literally borne out by history. The valour and conduct of Corbulo had placed Tigranes on the throne of Armenia, as the vassal of Rome. Suetonius Paulinus had completely subdued the rebellion in Britain, by the defeat of Boadicea and her daughters on the plains of Verulam; the Batavians and other tribes in the north of Germany were kept in check by the legions under Paulinus and Vetus; and the Jewish insurrection, that terminated in the destruction of Jerusalem, had not yet broken out.

[o] Page 61. Tacitus' *Annals*, xv. 44.

[p] Page 62. This was the opinion entertained of the Jews by the Romans at that time.— See Tacitus' account of it in his *History*, Bk. v., sec. 5.

^q Page 62. "Dost thou appeal unto Cæsar? unto Cæsar shalt thou go."—Acts xxv. 12.

^r Page 62. Tacitus' *Annals*, xv. 44.

^s Page 63. Acts xviii. 2; also Suetonius' *Life of Claudius*. Whether the edict ceased with that Emperor's life, or was ever repealed, is uncertain; but true it is, that upon St. Paul's arrival at Rome, he found a great number of Jews there, with whom the Christians were identified.—See last chapter of the Acts of the Apostles.

^t Page 64. St. Paul's Epistle to the Romans, xiii. 1.

^u Page 65. "This thou knowest, that all they which are in Asia be turned away from me; of whom are Phygellus and Hermogenes."—2 Tim. i. 15.

^v Page 65. The terms impostor, villain, and viper, used by Nero to St. Paul, are warranted by the authorities of the ancient Fathers.—See Cave's *Life of St. Paul*.

^w Page 67. "What will this babbler say?"—Acts xvii. 18.

^x Page 68. "Alexander the coppersmith did me much evil."—2 Tim. iv. 14. This is supposed by commentators to be the same Alexander mentioned in Acts xix. 33, who encountered St. Paul at Ephesus.

^y Page 69. Junius Gallio was the brother of the famous Seneca, and Proconsul of Achaia, of which Corinth was the capital, and is the same Gallio mentioned in Acts xviii. 12, 17.

^z Page 70. One of the earliest calumnies against the Christians was, that they were in the habit of sacrificing a child to their tutelar deity: and the author submits that this might have had its foundation in some renegade Christians imperfectly reporting to their ignorant heathen brethren the rite of Baptism, as that of the Lord's Supper gave rise, in a similar manner, to their eating human flesh.

^{aa} Page 72. The miracles of our Saviour and His apostles were attributed by the heathen to magic—an art in great vogue in that age of spiritual darkness.

^{bb} Page 73. The Consulate of the Emperor Claudius for the second time, and C. Licinius Cæcina Largus, corresponds with the forty-second year of our era, when Barnabas and Paul first visited Cyprus.

^{cc} Page 73.   Acts of the Apostles, xiii. 6—12.

^{dd} Page 75.   The name of one of the principal prisons in Rome.

^{ee} Page 75.   Tacitus' *Annals*, xv. 44.

Page 75.   This is in strict accordance with ecclesiastical history, as well as the customs of the Romans, who never suffered a citizen to be put to death but by the sword: and that St. Paul was a Roman citizen we have his own words recorded in Acts xxii. 25: " Is it lawful for you to scourge a man that is a Roman, and uncondemned?"

^{gg} Page 75.   See Tacitus' *Annals*, xiv. 53.

^{hh} Page 76.   This is distinctly asserted by Justyn Martyr, and Tertullian, in their Apologies, the first addressed to the Emperor Antoninus Pius, the second to the Emperor Severus.

ⁱⁱ Page 76.   It was the custom of all Roman Governors to record their Acts, and at the termination of their government to transmit them to Rome, there to be kept with other archives in the Capitol.   The Acts of Pilate are cited by Eusebius in his *Ecclesiastical History*, in proof of the truth of the Christian religion.

^{jj} Page 76.   This was the mode the Romans had of detecting Christians.—See Pliny's *Letter to Trajan*.

^{kk} Page 78.   Tacitus' *Annals*, xv. 44.

BOOK IV.

—

PAUL'S VISION.

— ◦ —

ARGUMENT.

PAUL, with his followers, the Christians, being condemned for setting Rome on fire, are confined in the Mamertine prison, prior to their execution, when he takes occasion to relate to his fellow prisoners what occurred at the time of his miraculous conversion. Is snatched up to Heaven—Is permitted to see the wonders of the universe—Past, present, and future — Incomprehensible to human understanding. The Deity—His worship in Heaven. Paul's call to be an Apostle—Is shewn the origin of the earth—Its progression through successive ages to its present state—The inhabitants of the last world—The beautiful appearance of the new—Man created—His fall and redemption. Paul ordained to preach the Gospel—Is encouraged by a fore-knowledge of its success and the events that led to it—Its beginning and growth compared to a stream—Persecution favours it. The death of Nero—Contests for the Empire—Judæa—The revolt of the Jews—Agrippa's advice despised—Vespasian—Titus—Ignorant of the destinies they are about to fulfil. The horror of war—Jotapata besieged—Josephus compelled to surrender—Dreadful determination and obstinacy of the Jews—Is carried before Vespasian—His lofty and remarkable appearance—His life spared by Vespasian at the intercession of Titus—Foretells their elevation to the purple—Their sensations thereon—Vespasian's departure—Josephus' close alliance with Titus. Jerusalem —Its famous antiquity and renown—The last refuge of the Jews—Its execrable tyrants—Its doom pronounced by a maniac.

PAUL'S VISION.

"Inde toro páter Æneas sic orsus ab alto."—VIRGIL'S ÆNEID, lib. ii.

THE closing bolts throughout the gaol resound,[a]
When in a spacious dungeon gather round,
In mark'd obedience and in silence all,
The doom'd associates of their teacher Paul;
Who to prepare them for their coming fate,
Does thus his promis'd narrative relate.

My fellow prisoners, brothers in the Lord,
Ye true believers in His holy Word,
If verging on eternity I shew
The revelations you desire to know;—
If I of unknown wonders dare to speak,
Remember, I, like mortal flesh, am weak;
Remember, too, to mortals 'tis not given
To comprehend the ways of God in heaven:
'Tis in the spirit only you shall see
The wondrous things that were reveal'd to me;
'Twas in the spirit I was snatch'd from earth,
And in the spirit I receiv'd my birth"—
My birth in Christ, which I before did shew
To Felix, Festus, King Agrippa too;

When I at Cæsarea first was bound
For preaching Him whose grace ye all have found,
And which beloved Luke has writ for those
Who seek the fountain whence His mercy flows.^c

 But think not you my vision ended here—
Think not, because my soul was smit with fear,
And to all those around I did appear
As stunn'd and senseless when to earth I fell,
I saw and heard no more :—Oh ! no; the spell
Was lengthen'd after this ; for He that cried
" Saul, Saul," unseen continued by my side,
And wafted me in silence to the sky,
Where worlds on worlds in endless motion fly,
Swifter than thought, and countless as the sand
All oceans' waters leave upon the strand,
Where Space is boundless, and where Time's no more ;
Where Present, Past, and Future to explore,
Is given to all who through those regions soar.

 'Tis this Almighty prescience that confounds
Our finite understanding, and sets bounds
To human reason, its appetence, and all
That raises man above the things that crawl ;
Makes him aspire to more than mortal ken—
Sinks him beneath the meanest insect when—
His feeble faculties he dare compare
With Him supreme—the Lord of earth and air—
The world's sole Architect—the great First Cause—
The Source divine—the God of Nature's laws.

Seraphic chorus to their heavenly King
Ten thousand times ten thousand angels sing,
From every part, from every voice arise,
Worship and praise to Him above the skies:—
Hosannas, glory, honour and renown,
Peal through the vault of heaven to the crown
Worn by eternal Majesty divine,
Who makes the ample universe His shrine.

Amazed, astounded, with what there I saw,
Some powerful impulse urged me to withdraw;
Stain'd with mortality, I could not mix
With things immortal, or mine eyes could fix
On aught celestial; for attraction strong,
My spirit drew insensibly along
To where this earth, expanded to my view,
A scene presented to my senses new.

The Voice then said—" No longer Saul, but Paul,"
" For so henceforward all mankind shall call
" The man selected out of common course
" My Name to publish, and the truth enforce.
" Now mark me Paul; to thee 'tis given to see
" Into the secrets of futurity:—
" Why of all others I have chosen thee,
" Who from the first hast persecuted me;
" Hast dealt out death, destruction unto all
" My true disciples and hast caused their fall,
" Thou question not:—suffice it is His will,
" With this my Gospel the whole earth to fill;

" Behold the Past, what Moses writ is true,
" And each succeeding cycle thou shalt view."

Then with what wonders was my soul embued,
E'en the remotest past could not elude
My comprehensive sight;—whirled round the Sun,
By secret impetus its course to run,
A nebulosity—a heated mass,[e]
Shapeless and void before mine eyes did pass.[f]

Next came an orb of form exact and bright;
For He that framed it, said " Let there be light;"[g]
Then light first beamed upon this globe and caused
That glorious object that ne'er since has paused
To give to vegetation heat and life;
To rule the seasons, and make all things rife
With plenteous increase—kind producing kind
In regular rotation.   Still we find
All issuing from Him who spake the word
" Let there be light!" and Sun and Moon occurr'd.

It came again—a pure transparent air
The globe encircled—blended with the care
To order due; that order Nature's law,
And it the first the God of Nature saw.
This globe was aqueous, in the boundless deep,
Great whales and multitude of fishes keep;[h]
Shook from its centre by Divine command,
The seas divide, and then appeared the land.

When next it came—trees of enormous growth
Covered the land; sea and forest both[i]
With life are quite redundant :—fish, fowl, beast,
The globe inhabited, and mine eyes did feast
On all the wonders of a former world :[j]
Huge antler'd things, and monstrous reptiles curl'd
In deep and dark recesses, overgrown
With leaves gigantic, and dank weeds unknown.
All, all was strange, and all was on a scale
Of vast proportion, that I could not hail
One living thing by name, or plant by kind,[k]
Or call the like of any to my mind.

Amphibious animals of bulk immense,[l]
From out some mighty stream led by the sense
Of powerful instinct, wade to the steepy bank,
Where pasture wild, exuberant and rank,
Invite the monster's appetite; while he,
His arched horns embracing some huge tree,
Grazes his fill; winged creatures wake the air,
With flight and flap incessant :—rivers bear[m]
Stupendous tribes, who with extended jaws,
And limbs that serve for paddles or for claws,
Await their prey :—on the shore are seen[n]
Unsightly bodies, loathsome and unclean :[o]
While in mid heaven thus allowed to poise,
Mine ears assail'd with most discordant noise,
Some great convulsion, plunged in one abyss,
The vermins croak—the flying serpents hiss.[p]

Last the new world, the new creation came,
Which Wisdom Infinite alone could frame,
From out the wreck of others gone before,
The first,—of this, and all Progenitor:
Order and law in every thing He did
Order and law from man's observance hid.[q]

Fresh from its Maker's hands it looked a gem
All sorts of gems comprising;—chief 'mong them,
The emerald with the sapphire interlaid,
While here and there the yellow topaze stray'd;
Onyx and blushing amethyst between,
Ruby and jardine stone distinctly seen;
Diamonds at either point encased in gold,
Radiant and lustrous, as it onward roll'd;
Emitting corruscations in the sky,
Of every hue such splendid gems supply:
Proofs of magnificence and sublimity!
Worthy the glory of the Deity.[r]

Oceans whereon the Sun for ever gleams,
Lakes that reflect the Moon's soft silvery beams,
Islands and continents with verdant plains,
And fruitful forests thick,—where like the veins,
That intersect the human body, flow
Rivers and streams that nourish as they go;
(Save trackless deserts, burning mountains, where
With icy poles, His bounty cannot share;)
Are all replete with life; earth, air and sea,
Yielding those living things God said should be.

While thus I pondered o'er this wondrous change,
While with delighted soul mine eye would range,
O'er all the works creation's power displayed,
Where birds in brightest plumage were arrayed,
In colours brilliant as the sun-lit flowers,
That spring spontaneous from their native bowers ;—
Or where their warbling, mellow notes abound,
Raising in concert one harmonious sound ;—
Where graceful animals of varied race,
Bound o'er the plain, or through the forest pace ;—
Where speckled tenants down the rivers glide,
And shoals of fishes swarm the briny tide ;—
Where insects glitter on the fragile leaf,
With form as buoyant, and with life as brief :—
While thus these altered wonders I survey'd,
The Voice that twice before had spoken, said—

    " Paul, thou hast seen what things have passed
        away,
" What changes wrought by His eternal sway,
" To whom ten thousand years are as a day ;[s]
" And now, this globe prepared for man's abode,
" God called him into life :—not in the mode
" He now exists ; but in that perfect state
" Angels enjoyed before the heavenly gate :
" Wisdom and goodness all His works pervade,
" And all things for the use of man were made ;
" Dominion over all He freely gave,
" And crowned with bliss, He left him nought to
        crave ;[t]

" Endowed with reason, man was free to act.

" And man's obedience all He did exact :

" Why ill was suffered to contend with good,

" Why Satan the Almighty's will withstood,

" Resisting still the arm that thrust him forth

" From Heaven, and tried his subtlety on earth,

" Thou must not know :—by disobedience fell

" Man from his height ;—the rest the Scriptures tell.

" The Present mark—His promise to fulfil,

" When man abandoned to his own free will,

" From paradise expelled, brought down the curse,

" I,—pre-ordain'd that sentence to reverse,

" Reclaim, redeem his offspring, from the past,

" O'er my divinity the garment cast

" Of frail mortality, on earth appeared,

" And suffer'd death,—a Sacrifice that cleared

" Man of his sin ;—on that my Gospel reared

" Those hopes of heaven,—that my first martyrs cheered."

" Its growth successful,—thou already knowst,

" And with perverted zeal, hast made thy boast,

" How thou didst punish, persecute and vex

" My faithful followers of either sex :

" But thinkst vain man that thou canst contravene

" The will of God ;—when thy poor feeble spleen,

" Promotes the culture of the truth divine,

" Defeats thy purpose, and advances mine :

" The means by Him employed, man heeds not of ;

" And lured by Satan, stoops to rail and scoff :

" The hearts of all men He does so permit,

" 'Twixt good and ill to choose, as they think fit ;—

" With mind to guide :—then turn thee from thy course,
" And let thy faith henceforward be the source
" Of all thine energies ;—that faith in me
" That bringeth man to blessed eternity :
" For though thou'st been an instrument for ill,
" Behold it worketh the Almighty's will :
" My Gospel to Jerusalem confined,
" On Stephen's death, with other acts combined,
" Some true disciples to Damascus drove, ᵂ
" And divers cities, where they fearless strove
" To testify of me, to preach the Word,
" To teach the doctrine which from me they heard :—
" That doctrine now demands thine utmost zeal,
" Its truth to propagate, its force to feel ;
" To spread through distant nations, and to vie
" With my first followers in variety
" Of hardship, suffering, duresse, and the like,
" With which 't shall please the Almighty them to
          strike.
" Thee to encourage in this new belief,
" For 'twill be one of anguish, toil and grief ;—
" Thou art permitted the success to know,
" Shall crown thine efforts in the world below ;
" But lest from this, presumption thou may'st find,
" And drive humility from out thy mind ;—
" Bear with thee this ;—in pain remember me,
" Infirm of speech and maimed shalt thou be." ˣ

Here ceased the Voice :—before me then was spread
The future progress of our faith, that led

Through trains and labyrinths of mystic power,
To this eventful, this predestin'd hour:
My life foretold, 'twere needless to relate,
Well known to you, as this my present state:
But to enable you, my friends, to meet
That coming fate, to-morrow may complete,
Your faith to strengthen, should it strength require,
With hope your parting spirits to inspire,—
With constancy and courage to defy,—
The tyrant's torments and in Christ to die:
I,—to your longing ears will now unfold,
What there an Angel gave me to behold;
Restrain your wonder then, while I relate,
What yet is hidden in the book of fate.

The tyrant's death the first event I saw,
His crimes outstripping God's and human law,
Provoke the Senate 'gainst him to conspire;
Enraged, incensed, escaping from their ire;—
Disgraced, disguised, a hated wretch he flies,—
Disowned, despised, a recreant coward dies:
And to posterity hands down a name,
That men will execrate, and dogs will shame.[y]

Then shall our faith spread o'er this Empire's rule,
To Gaul, Spain, Britain, e'en to utmost Thule,[z]
It now extends;—and penetrating wide,
Nor seas nor mountains shall its force abide.
As from some hidden, some untrodden spot,
Where sacred silence reigns within her grot;

Some streamlet takes its earthborn bubbling rise,
And issues forth with scarce a murmur's noise,
Steals through the glen, unnoticed winds along,
In breadth increasing, till it meets some strong,
Some high embankment, or some deep ravine :
When rushing, through, above, below, between,
Its waters sever, overflow the land,
And renders that, before a barren sand,
A soil prolific :—teeming with the vine,
With oil and corn, with flocks and lowing kine :
Meeting below, it gathers greater strength
From each successive hindrance : till at length
A peerless river rolls its waters on,
Superb, majestic,—all prevention gone ;
Diffusing health and wealth where'er it flows,
Defying further hindrance from its foes.
So persecution shall our creed advance,
So death and torment shall our faith enhance ;
And every unborn tyrant that his sword,
Against the followers of Christ's holy word
Shall ruthless draw, its progress to prevent,
Will only serve its durance to cement."

To this succeeds commotion, bloodshed, strife ;
Intestine warfare, waste of human life,—
Involve the Roman world ;—chief after chief
Contending for the Empire, give relief
To all whose future hopes on Christ are laid,
And persecution for awhile is stayed.

But in Judæa what do I descry,—
The Roman eagles from the Province fly ;
Oppression's wrongs no longer to be borne,
The vanquish'd on the victors turn with scorn ;
Further subjection they with force repel,
For blood insatiate,—they in arms rebel ;
Met by o'erpowering numbers of the Jews,
The first attack,—the Roman legions lose ;
Success intoxicates, and every tribe,
Revenge and hate to Roman sway imbibe :[cc]
In vain Agrippa pleads the Roman name,
Numbers of legions, discipline and fame,
Extent of Empire,—power on sea and land,
And powerful nations under their command ;
In vain implores their rash resolve to cease,
To throw aside their arms and sue for peace :
Agrippa's speech does but their wrath provoke,
Revolt, revolt,—throw off the Roman yoke !
Is all the cry :—it spreads through city, plain,
O'er hill and vale, and reaches to the main.[dd]

And on that main the Roman navy rides,
With vet'ran troops, from distant Britain's tides ;
While he their chief, who Britain's sons subdued,
Again to conquer is with power endued :
On Egypt's sands I see the warlike man,
In Rome yclept renowned Vespasian ;[ee]
For skill in arms, throughout the Empire known,
That Empire shortly destined for his own ;

His army marshal'd on the dusty plain,—
He seeks not now their confidence to gain;
But through their ranks I see him proudly ride,
In earnest converse mounted by his side,
On barbed charger of Numidian breed,
Famed for their strength, their courage and their
      speed,
A form erect, bare headed: he is eyed
By all the soldiers,—as they view with pride
The graceful forehead and the visage bland,
Where force and intellect go hand in hand,
Where quick determination takes its stand,
A warrior formed by nature to command:"
His name along the ranks, loud echo brings
And "Titus, Titus," in the welkin rings.
Courteous to all, with smiles his thanks he tends :—
Tumultuous praise from all the host ascends :
Proud of that host, still prouder of his son,
The chief advances, and the war's begun.

Vain pomp of mortals! insects as you seem,
And in your earthly glory only dream
Of martial honours, or the mural crown,
Won with the spoils of some besieged town ;
With captive chiefs and pris'ners in your train,
When Rome, in splendid triumph you regain ;
You little know what destinies you hold,
What sacred truths your valour shall unfold :—
Th' Almighty's vengeance now it is you bear,
To hurl on those whose bitter hatred dare,

When Pilate would the Holy Jesus save,
With taunts and oaths and imprecations rave :—
" On us and on our children be His blood"[ss]—
Must now be answered, and it seemeth good
To His Almighty wisdom to design,
You, to inflict the punishment divine.

War, dreadful war, now rages through the land,
The Jews, their foes not able to withstand,
(For valour, fame, and discipline unite,
Their wilder rage and fury to requite ;)
The plains and hilly country soon forsake,
To towers and forts, and fenced cities take :
In fight unequal,—they for refuge fly,
Unyielding yet, defensive war to try :
But vain their efforts, vain their utmost skill,
'Gainst veteran legions, purposed to fulfil,
With dauntless courage, what their chief directs,
Reckless of all but what his fame affects :
Bravely defended, all will not avail,
The towers they undermine, the walls they scale,
And entering in with carnage fill the town :
Slavery and death the victors' fury crown.[hh]

First Gadara, then Jotapata falls ;
But in the last, the chief upon the walls,
In fight courageous, and in counsel wise,
With matchless ingenuity supplies
The Jews with new device to counteract
Their fierce endeavours, and the siege protract ;—

Till by a faithless follower in the night,
The foe's admitted ;—not for safety, flight,
The Jews now strive,—but slaughtered in the streets
Breathing defiance, each his death-wound meets.[ii]

So in some pathless forest you may see,
Where beasts ferocious roam at liberty ;
Intent on blood, their sides each other rend ;—
When for some new-found carcase they contend,
With threat'ning growl and flashing eye they dart,—
In fervent hate's embrace ;—and never part
Till one,—with breath and strength exhausted lies,—
The other worn and lacerated dies.

Oh ! when will man such mortal strife forego !
When will he seek his loftier state to know !
When will he cease to imitate the brute,
And from his breast destructive passions root ;
Render this earth, where might be happiness,
A world of woe, a moral wilderness !

Meantime the Jewish leader in a cave,
Whose foes would spare not, nor his friends would
        save,
Is by an unseen Providence preserved,[ii]
By His Almighty prescience reserved,
To give to future ages record true,
Of that dire judgment, he himself should view :
Through crowds of soldiers he is borne along,
In bonds—a captive ; while the clamorous throng

Shout, some for instant death, and some deride
His fallen fortune.   With becoming pride
He walks unmindful of the vulgar cry,
Wearing an air of conscious dignity :
There was a mark'd expression on his brow—
More often used to order, than to bow—
As now he does, at great Vespasian's feet,
And for a private audience does entreat :
His sorrowing aspect and his flowing beard,
In one whose prowess they so lately fear'd,
Begets commiseration in the breast
Of each and all :—young Titus 'bove the rest
In pity with his father intercedes,
And for the life of famed Josephus pleads—
The Jewish chief, the warrior, the priest,
And of God's chosen seers, not the least.[kk]

In speech prophetic, he at once declares
The Purple vacant and the Empire theirs :
The father first,—and then the aspiring son
He hails as Cæsar, ere the title's won :
Such great advancement, such exalted rank,
Foretold so gravely, when as yet no blank
In the Imperial dynasty is seen,
The sire in thought confounds ;—his rigid mien[ll]
Suffused,—betrays emotions of the heart,
That strange forebodings ever will impart ;
In silent consternation he is lost,
His mind 'twixt doubt and expectation toss'd :

Not so with Titus, his dilating eye,
And cheeks that glowed with inborn energy ;—
His veneration for the suppliant Jew,
Evinced that he receives the words as true ;
Impressed with awe he cannot understand,
In earnest pledge he tenders him his hand ;
From thence esteems Josephus as a friend,
With whom henceforth his destiny must blend : [mm]
Honour'd by both, but ever on his guard,
The wary chieftain keeps him still in ward.

The secret conclave rise,—the war's renewed,—
And Joppa, Gamala, are in turn subdued :
Judæa won,—the Roman ensigns wave
O'er tower and fort, and every city, save
Jerusalem !—The chosen spot of God,
Where Abraham offered and where Isaac trod, [nn]
Where Jacob slept and dreamed of things above,
Of angels' visits, and Jehovah's love : [oo]
Jerusalem !—Where royal David strung,
Inspired by God, the holy songs he sung ;
Where Solomon beloved of God, upreared
That sacred fabric, to all Jews endeared :
Jerusalem !— Where Jesus wept and taught,
And where the Son of man his wonders wrought ;
Where malice over innocence prevailed ;
When to the cross the Lord of Life they nailed :
Jerusalem !—The refuge and the den
Of hostile factions, and bloodthirsty men ;

The dwelling-place of dæmons, who excel,
In crime and blasphemy, the sons of hell. ᴾᴾ

Oh! wretched city! glutted with the gore
Of mutual slaughter, how often did of yore
The holy prophets warn thee of these times,
And threaten retribution for thy crimes!
Oh! wicked people! who could e'er surmise,
The ties of kindred thus ye would despise,
And on each other vent the tiger's rage,
A bloody war exterminating wage:
Famine and murder thro' the city stalk,
Lust, rapine, misery, together walk;
Three tyrants cruel, merciless and vile,
Remorseless, exercise with serpent's guile,
The sway of dæmons, each surpassing each,
In dev'lish revelry,—in satanic breach
Of every law should regulate the soul,
Confounding in iniquity the whole.

Yet is thy doom deferred, thy final doom,—
Ere yet the sacred Temple 's made the tomb,
Of ancient splendour and of holy rites,
Is for a while withheld:—for Rome invites
Judæa's victor to the vacant throne,
And he prepares to challenge it alone:
Vespasian now the Roman sceptre wields,
The Roman world to him obedience yields;
Permitted but to see Jerusalem's walls,
Imperial duties for his presence calls:

From the rebellious city he departs,
But ere he goes, to Titus he imparts
His full conviction, some all-ruling power
Had destined him for Empire,—from the hour
Josephus prophesied in terms sublime,
Events that slumbered in the womb of time ;—
But briefly slumbered, for a speedy birth
Gives to his words integrity and worth :
" And is it just," I hear him say, " to see
" Such holy man deprived of liberty ;
" Would 't not, my Titus, more exalt our fame,
" At once to banish such reproach and shame ?"

Into their presence then the prisoner's brought,
His looks, his words, with eager survey sought :
The truthful glance, the proud and peerless nod,
Tells them he came a messenger from God :
His bonds they cut in pieces, and requite[m]
With princely favours, his prophetic sight ;
The sire bestows, the son with joy receives,
In firm alliance, one whom he believes,
Endowed with mind superior from on high,—
Ordained by God his counsel to supply :
In the fulfilment of the sacred word,
That gives the Holy City to the sword,
Of Gentile nations and a Roman Lord.[n]

As when the heavens lower on the plain,
And inky clouds portend the coming rain,

The beasts for shelter to the covert run,
In vain the angry elements to shun,
For certain death awaits them from the storm,
Where trees attract the forked lightning's form :
So from the towns the fugitives repair,
The faint, the strong, the squalid and the fair,
For safety, succour, to their only home,
The last sad refuge from revengeful Rome,—
To where their fate 's completed, for they stay
To fall in heaps, an almost countless prey.

And who their melancholy entrance greets ?
Who their despondence with despondence meets ?
With rueful visage, and with mournful voice,
A maniac bids them never more rejoice :
" Woe to Jerusalem !"—he loudly cries,
As through the streets with hurried step he hies :
" Woe to Jerusalem !" nought else is heard ;
" Woe to Jerusalem !"—no other word
Escapes his lips ;—perambulating wide,
These doleful notes attend his every stride :
" Woe to Jerusalem !" nought else he says,
This lonely presage takes up all his days ;
In vain the people tempt with offers kind,
In vain with thongs his hands and feet they bind ;
They promise, threaten, punish and entreat,
And now they fain would feast, and now they beat :
While with vindictive spleen, the scourge they ply,
To every lash, he iterates the cry ;

No force can stop him—no allurements gain—
No earthly power his warning voice restrain :
Still he repeats, despite or friend or foe,
" Woe to Jerusalem !"   " To Jerusalem woe ! "[88]

END OF THE FOURTH BOOK.

NOTES TO BOOK IV.

^a Page 84. The Mamertine; one of the principal prisons in Rome, where it is supposed St. Paul was confined with the other Christians condemned to suffer by Nero for the conflagration. —See Tacitus' *Annals*, B. xvi. to xliv.

^b Page 84. "I knew a man in Christ above fourteen years ago (whether in the body I cannot tell; or whether out of the body I cannot tell); how that he was caught up into paradise, and heard unspeakable words."—2 Cor. xii. 2, 3, 4. Does not the Apostle here speak of himself?

^c Page 85. Acts of the Apostles, xxiii. xxiv. xxv.

^d Page 86. The learned commentators have assigned various reasons for the transformation of the name of the great Apostle immediately after his conversion; but all must be conjecture, as the sacred historian only mentions the fact. "Then Saul who is also called Paul."—Acts xiii. 9.

^e Page 87. See Professor Sedgwick's Discourse before the University, published in 1834, page 28 ; a work that should be read by all who would not have their faith shaken or their reason subdued by modern science, but the one confirmed and the other exalted.

^f Page 87. "And the earth was without form, and void." Genesis i. 2.

^g Page 87. "And God said, Let there be light : and there was light."—Genesis i. 3.

^h Page 87. "And God created great whales, and every living creature that moveth, which the waters brought forth abundantly, after their kind."—Genesis i. 21.

ⁱ Page 88. It will be observed by the preceding note, that fish was the first part of the animal creation ; a proof that at that time the globe was entirely of water or moving sand, and it was not till some following convulsion that there was any land. "And God said, Let

the waters under the heaven be gathered together unto one place, and let the dry land appear."—Genesis i. 9.

ʲ Page 88. The attempt here made by the author to reconcile the discoveries that the science of Geology has already made with the historical account of the creation transmitted to us by the inspired Word of God through the Jewish lawgiver is somewhat justified by "Sermons in Stones,' and may not be unacceptable to the sincere believer.

ᵏ Page 88. There have been no real fossils yet discovered that have relation in comparative anatomy to any of the present animal creation.

ˡ Page 88. The immense frame, or skeleton, exhibited by Mr. Catlin, the celebrated American traveller, at the Egyptian Hall, gives a good idea of some of the inhabitants of a former world.

ᵐ Page 88. The Draco volens, or flying serpent.

ⁿ Page 88. The Ichthyosaurus or Plethyosaurus, specimens of which are to be seen in the British Museum and elsewhere; one in excellent preservation in the University Collection at Cambridge, which was found on the estate of the late W. Layton, Esq., at Chettisham, near Ely, when making a cutting for the Ely and Peterborough Railway.

ᵒ Page 88. For these and other remains of a former world, see the Discourses of Cuvier, Buckland, Sedgwick, and others.

ᵖ Page 88. The great progress made in the science of Chemistry seems to assure us, that the last revolution our planet underwent was caused by internal combustion, and therefore was as sudden as it was complete.

ᑫ Page 89. The science of Geology being quite unknown, and that of Chemistry but half understood, by the ancients, they would not possibly calculate upon the order of events now so apparent to the studious philosopher; all of which must confirm him in the belief in a pre-existing Supreme Power, an Almighty, Omniscient, and Immutable God. "Before the mountains were brought forth, or ever the earth and the world were made, Thou art God, from everlasting, and world without end."—Psalm xc. 2.

ʳ Page 89. The illustrations here attempted will be considered a great stretch of the imagination, or a poor, sorry, and imperfect effort of fancy,—but were it possible to bring what might be the semblance of this globe in an inverted ratio to the capacity of human optics, it may not seem quite so preposterous when connected with the ensuing development.

ˢ Page 90. " For a thousand years in Thy sight are but as yesterday, seeing that it passes as a watch in the night."—Psalm xc. 4.

ᵗ Page 90. See the second chapter of the Book of Genesis, more particularly the last verse, which may be taken as conclusive of the perfect bliss of our first parents.

ᵘ Page 91. "But he, being full of the Holy Ghost, looked up stedfastly into heaven, and saw the glory of God, and Jesus standing on the right hand of God, and said, Behold, I see the heavens opened, and the Son of man standing on the right hand of God."—Acts vii. 55, 56.

ᵛ Page 91. "As for Saul, he made havoc of the church, entering into every house; and haling men and women, committed them to prison."—Acts viii. 3.

ʷ Page 92. "And Saul yet breathing out threatenings and slaughter against the disciples of the Lord, went unto the high priest, and desired of him letters to Damascus."—Acts ix. 1, 2.

ˣ Page 92. Taking for granted the vision the Apostle alluded to in the twelfth chapter of the Second Epistle to the Corinthians is cotemporary with his conversion, we are led to believe he was struck with some sudden affection of the mental organs, and, to the appearance of the bystanders, he was in a fit ; for upon the re-entrance of the spirit into the flesh—that is, upon his recovery—he ever afterwards shewed strong evidence of having been smitten with paralysis. "And lest I should be exalted above measure through the abundance of the revelations, there was given to me a thorn in the flesh, the messenger of Satan, to buffet me, lest I should be exalted above measure." —2 Cor. xii. 7. It should be observed here, that so convinced is the Apostle of the cause and necessity of his afflictions, that he mentions them both at the beginning and the end of the same verse.

ʸ Page 93. The life, death, and government of the execrable tyrant Nero are so minutely related by Tacitus, that the classical reader need only refer to his elegant pages for the truth of the historical facts here so briefly enumerated.

ᵃ Page 93. By the time of the martyrdom of St. Paul, the Gospel had been preached in all the countries named, and, as some assert, by the great Apostle himself and his associates. Thule, otherwise Thulé, the Ireland of us moderns, was the land to which he crossed from Spain previous to his visit to Britain and his return to Rome through Gaul.—See Moore's *History of Ireland*.

ᵃᵃ Page 94. That the growth of Christianity was not retarded by any one of the great persecutions related by the Fathers we have sufficient proof in the history of the Church and the writings of the ancients, beginning at the Acts of the Apostles.

ᵇᵇ Page 94. The civil wars the death of Nero gave rise to drew men's attention from the still, but rapid, progress Christianity was making during the short and turbulent reigns of Galba, Otho, and Vitellius, as well as the more peaceful government of Vespasian and Titus.

ᶜᶜ Page 95. For the cause of the insurrection of the Jews, see Josephus' *Wars of the Jews*, Book ii.

ᵈᵈ Page 95. Also, Agrippa's speech, and its result.

ᵉᵉ Page 95. *Josephus*, Book iii. ch. 1. Also, Suetonius' *Life of Vespasian*.

ᶠᶠ Page 96. Suetonius' *Life of Titus*; also, his description and character.

ᵍᶻ Page 97. "Then answered all the people and said, His blood be upon us, and on our children."—St. Matthew xxvii. 25.

ʰʰ Page 97. The brave and obdurate resistance made by the Jews in the different fortified places to which they had retired on the advance of Vespasian with his army so enraged the Roman soldiery, that they gave no quarter; nor did the Jews ask it, in any of their cities taken by assault.—Josephus' *Wars*.

ⁱⁱ Page 98. The city of Jotapata was defended by Josephus in person; the siege, its ingenious mode of defence, its final capture by treachery, is therefore most minutely described by the warrior and historian. See his *Wars of the Jews*, Book iii. ch. 7.

ʲʲ Page 98. The almost miraculous preservation of Josephus is beautifully observed upon by Benson.—*Hulsean Lectures*, vol. i., disc. x.

[kk] Page 99. Although out of the pale of sacred historians, Josephus must be considered as somewhat differing from those of his own age; his subject, the Siege of Jerusalem in particular, forming the connecting link between sacred and profane history.

[ll] Page 99. Vespasian was noted for the harshness or rigidity of his features.—*Suetonius.*

[mm] Page 100. The reception of Josephus by Titus after his capture—(considering the slaughter he had made of the Roman soldiers, almost involving the death of Vespasian—his pardon and subsequent admission into the councils of the Roman chief—the firm friendship established between them)—may be attributed to an all-wise and overruling Providence.

[nn] Page 100. "Take now thy son, thine only son Isaac, whom thou lovest, and get thee into the land of Moriah; and offer him there for a burnt-offering upon one of the mountains which I will tell thee of."—Gen. xxii. 2.

[oo] Page 100. "And he dreamed, and, behold, a ladder set up on the earth, and the top of it reached to heaven: and, behold, the angels of God ascending and descending on it."—Gen. xxviii. 12.

[pp] Page 101. Some opinion may be formed of the different epochs of the Holy City as well from Josephus as from Scripture.

[qq] Page 102. It was the custom of the Romans, when a prince or chief taken in arms was to be pardoned or liberated, to have him brought before the whole army, when a lictor, or officer specially appointed for the purpose, would with an axe or other instrument separate every link of the chain wherewith he was bound.—Adams's *Roman Antiquities.*

[rr] Page 102. "And Jerusalem shall be trodden down of the Gentiles."—St. Luke xxi. 24.

[ss] Page 104. Josephus is very particular and clear in his relation of this remarkable occurrence in the siege of the Holy City.—*Wars of the Jews*, Book vi. ch. v. sec. 3.

BOOK V.

—

PAUL'S VISION.

THE DESTRUCTION OF JERUSALEM.

———◆———

ARGUMENT.

PAUL's lamentation over the city—The Camp at Cæsarea—The Halls there. Titus—Bereniceé. Their march to Jerusalem. Antiochus —Pompey the Great—The Jews form an ambush. Titus' miraculous escape. Arrives before Jerusalem. Accompanied by Bereniceé and Josephus, surveys the beauty and strength of the City and the Temple. Forms his camp on the site of the Assyrians—Battles without the walls—Great numbers of the Jews crucified—Josephus would persuade the Jews to capitulate, but in vain—Is struck with a stone from the walls and stunn'd—Titus resolves to surround the City with a wall— Commences from the Camp of the Assyrians. Crosses the road to Emmaus. The two disciples—Gethsemané—Mount of Olives—Siloam —The Fountain—Pompey's Camp—Herod's Palace—The Wise Men —The slaughter of the Innocents—John the Baptist—Calvary. The wall completed—Enormities committed by the Jews—Famine, its dreadful effects. Paul's spirit troubled—Subdued by a voice. The fight renewed—The tower of Antonia partly demolished. The dead bodies cause a pestilence. A Heathen's prayer. A Council of War— Josephus and Nicanor wounded—The Temple converted into a citadel —Titus resolves to storm it—His speech to the soldiers—Bereniceé's address—The Romans repulsed—Titus sets fire to the gates—Terrible carnage of the Jews—A Roman soldier sets fire to the Temple—Titus' fruitless endeavours to stop the fire. The Holy of Holies—Its final destruction with the Temple.

THE DESTRUCTION OF JERUSALEM.

On ! ill-starr'd city, how shall I relate
The woe, the misery of thy coming fate !
When was such dreadful visitation known !
When more did Satan triumph o'er his own !
Too true the presage, true the maniac's cry,
Thy doom is seal'd in judgment from on high :
Unhappy Zion ! guilty to thy cost,
Thou hast been weighed, found wanting, and art lost :
Thy sons with thy destruction are inspired,
No Gentile foe, no Roman lord required :
Yet doth it please the Almighty now to send,
His instruments of wrath, with power to rend
The Temple's veil ;—the Temple too to burn ;
Uproot each stone,—and with the ploughshare turn
The sites and floors,—where stood thy holy walls,
To nurture weeds in desolation's halls.[a]

In Cæsarea's streets, the warlike tramp
Of men and horses, mark the Roman camp ;
Legions composed of nations from afar
All fired by hate,—all eager for the war :—
Allies and mercenaries, their standard join,
Rife with the hope of plunder, to purloin

The sacred treasure from the Holy place,
Where heaps on heaps, their fervid fancy trace.[b]

In Cæsarea's halls assemble now
Nobles and chieftains, princes who avow
Their firm allegiance to the Roman sway,
Proud such triumphant leaders to obey:
As in the forest stands some stately tree,
O'erlooking all with peerless majesty;
So Titas 'mong the glittering group appears,
The first in dignity, the last in years:
Scarce has he numbered thirty summers, though
A master-spirit all his actions shew:
Born to command, there sits upon his brow,
A mien, a soul, to which the loftiest bow:—
Fit instrument the Almighty's will to do,
Himself unconscious of the Godhead true:—
But not unconscious of His choicest gift,
Not free from passions, that his thoughts uplift
E'en from ambition;—power and fame apart,
He sues for love to Berenicé's heart:—
Nor vainly sues:—the proud imperious glance,
That would not favour e'en a king's advance;
Now yields to dictates that ennoble life,
Love for her country plunged in hopeless strife;
Her people writhing under Roman hate,
Invoke her aid, their doom to mitigate;
Pity and admiration fill her breast,
She smiles approval for her country's rest.[c]

I

Like Eve she's formed in Nature's finest mould,
With grace and dignity her sex t' uphold ;
And there's a heaven-born spirit dwells within,
That leads e'en Titus from the paths of sin—
Can truth impart, his heathen heart too guide,
To practise virtues, hitherto untried :
Well I remember that angelic look,
When Festus, with the king her brother, took
Counsel and thought, from one so grave, tho' young,
Wisdom distilled like honey from her tongue :
Oh ! bounteous Providence !   Oh ! beauteous sex !
Fair counterpart of manhood, that reflects
Man's sterner virtues, by the Almighty sent,
His cares to sooth, his sorrows to prevent :—
This talisman 'tis, that touches now his soul,
This powerful influence, does his mind control.

Richly caparison'd a war-horse waits,
To bear her proudly to Jerusalem's gates ;
By Titus' side,—in front of all the host,
Marshal'd in due array, she takes her post,
And on their march in fluent speech points out,
The various objects on the legion's route :
Mountains and plains could each a tale unfold,
Which she, with tearful reminiscence told ;
'Twas here Antiochus with war inflamed,[e]
Dominion o'er the Jewish nation claimed ;
'Twas there the Jews before great Pompey fled,
From Asia when his conquering arms he led ;

Pillage and massacre attend the Greek,
Woman and child in vain for mercy seek,
With blood of thousands plain and city reek :
Their laws he abrogates, with cruel spite,
Of circumcision he suspends the rite ;
Tortures their nobles,—priests and people slays,
In every act his vengeance he displays ;
With unclean animals their courts he soils,
Profanes their altars, and their Temple spoils :
Their holy Temple—Judah's pride and boast,
For splendour famed,—for purest worship most :
Not so the Roman,—his majestic mind,'
Bent upon conquest, but with mercy join'd,
Their laws respected,—left untouched their gold,
Their worship sanction'd, and at once enroll'd
In Rome's great commonwealth, the Jewish state,
A Roman Province henceforth was our fate.

As thus in pleasing colloquy they ride
Not heeding they, what dangers may betide,
Three noble chieftains mounted side by side ;
Followed by guards, who arm'd with sword and spear,
Leaving the host far distant in the rear :—
What clouds of dust full in their front arise !—
The Jews in ambush meditate surprise :—
Titus at once their wily object spies,
And to the head of chosen horsemen flies ;
One ardent glance on Berenicé turns,
Then to the friend who all his thoughts discerns,

"The Queen, Josephus, I commit to thee,—
"Placidus and Nicanor, follow me:"
Compact, in firm array, the Jews they met
Their first and furious charge, no fears beget:—
But steed to steed and hand to hand they fight,
While spears and arrows shower down their flight:
Titus—conspicuous from the rest afar,
Known by his helmless front amid the war,
Is all their aim:—Titus alive or dead,—
Hope of the Empire,—but their nation's dread,—
Once in their hands:—what may not then succeed:
The Romans vanquished, and Judæa freed.
Unbraced, unarmed, he seems an easy prey,
To those who plunge revengeful in the fray:
Around his head, the jav'lins harmless hiss,
His limbs and body, spear and faulchion miss,
Close by his side both friends and foemen lie,
Untouched his steed, when horse and rider die—
While with his naked arm, he deals around,
A hundred strokes, and every stroke a wound.⁸

While pondering o'er this deadly field, I saw,
How a sincere believer hence may draw,
A full assurance of Omniscient rule:
The hand Divine, is folly to the school
Of proud philosophy:—man marks not when
God's intervention is within his ken;
But all ascribes to chance:—to me revealed—
To them invisible—the sacred shield,

Held by an angel at the Lord's command
To save the chieftain from the vengeful band;
To turn the jav'lin's point, the arrow's flight,
From Titus' head, to some less glorious knight:
His chosen instrument, He screens from foes,
To 'complish that, which He to me foreshows."

Approached Jerusalem, his eye now roams
O'er modern palaces and ancient domes:
Her lofty towers and lengthened wall surveys,
While those her beauty, this her strength displays:
And as our holy Temple meets his sight,
His soul is wrapt in wonder and delight;
With awe-struck mind, its magnitude he views,
With saddened heart its coming fate he rues;
Recounts its ancient glories, which he learns
From Bereniçé and his friend by turns;
The last of Jewish worship would relate,
The first of Herod's and her grandsire's state;
What towers they built,—what courts, what gates adorn,
What treasure spent, when she was yet unborn:'
But neither spake of Him, whose voice had cried,
Against the Temple,—o'er its ruin sighed,—
Foretold its doom,—forewarned His followers meek,
To flee its precincts, and the desert seek:—
Its vast magnificence his soul inspires,[j]
Its old renown imagination fires,
To urge the siege,—the city to obtain,
And add fresh triumphs to Vespasian's reign.

On that same spot where the Assyrian host
In ages past, in one sad night were lost;
And left their camp, a monument of woe,
To heathen nations, and to Zion's foe;
He rears his standard:—no fear, no thought has he,
Of such o'erwhelming, dire catastrophe;
The God who once the city had preserved,
Deserts it now;—with sorrow I observed
The signal aid of His almighty arm,
Withdrawn,—transferred:—while terror and alarm
Pervade the Jews,—while their crimes ascend
And call for judgment,—guilty while they rend
All law divine and human, and all ties,
An angel o'er their city vengeful flies,
The angel of the Lord, the same that smote
Sennacherib's host, as erst the prophet wrote. [k]

'Twere vain to tell what horrors met mine eyes—
Horrors of war accumulating rise:
Without Jerusalem's walls, both sides display
Determined valour, and dispute each day;
The Romans now,—and now the Jews succeed,—
Death rules the combat, and both armies bleed:
Deceit and artifice attend the one,
Those meaner arts of war the Romans shun:
Vain, sinful men! your crimes are heard on high,
And you must reap the fruits of blasphemy;
Nor stratagem nor treachery can defraud,
Rome of her triumph, as decreed by God. [l]

Horror on horrors! round the walls I see,
Crosses unnumbered ;—on each fatal tree,
Writhing with torture, hangs a dying Jew,
Who suffers now, the death of Him they slew :
Just retribution on our nation falls,
Calvary,—now,—their punishment recalls :
I saw the avenging Angel's sword laid bare,
I heard his voice the wrath of God declare. ᵐ

Thus multitudes before the walls are slain,
And Titus with his legions, strives in vain
His eagles to advance beyond the plain :
Meanwhile Josephus with persuasive speech,
Would fain his wicked countrymen beseech
To cease rebellion, and for pardon ask,
When as he stops their leader's crimes to task ;
They hurl defiance at his sacred head,
Point with derision to the countless dead,
And under foot his proffered mercy tread :—
Nor this alone,—but aiming at his life,
Discharge a bolt with death and danger rife :
Senseless he falls, upon the ground o'erthrown,
The Jews in triumph shout,—and praise the stone,
That thus has laid their late commander low,
Their trait'rous chief, their proud, their bitterest foe.ⁿ

And now the chief protracted warfare spurns ;
He from his sire's, and own experience learns
A shorter mode, the city to subdue,—
A surer, safer conquest will ensue ;

If a strong outer wall beside their own,
His legions raise, and thus surround the town.

    First from the Assyrian's camp, his lines he draws"
To that frequented way,—the road t' Emmaus ;—
That sacred road,—trod by the Saviour's steps,
When He the two disciples intercepts ;
Who spake of Him and all His marv'lous deeds ;
Unknown to them, His voice He intercedes,
Explains, expounds the Scripture, and at last
Revealed Himself, and from their presence passed :
How beat their hearts in concert, when 'twas given
To them, to know the bonds of death were riven ;—
Their Lord restored to life,—His word fulfiled,"—
Their joy made perfect, and their doubting stilled :
So shall it be with us, when passing through
The gates of death, our spirits shall review,
Renew, His gracious promise and reward,
Those gifts, no earthly tyrant can retard.

    Thence to Gethsemané their lines they trace,
Where Kidron's brook, the Eastern walls embrace,
Facing the Temple, near that holy mount,
Scene of those wonders, tongue can scarce recount :
"Twas here the Saviour wept, 'twas there He prayed,
"Twas there He triumphed, and was here betrayed ;
There in transcendant 'fulgence 'twas He walked,
When He, with Moses and Elias talk'd ;
Close to the garden, where with bitterest gall,
His soul was smitten ;—they build up their wall ;

Nor deign to mark the spot, from whence He bid
Adieu to earth, and in the clouds was hid.
Glorious ascension! consummation great!
A boon mankind can never overrate!
Final accomplishment of that wise plan,
Ordained by God, to save, recover man.

Then to Siloam's tower the wall extends;
That fatal tower, that in its ruin blends,
A type of what our Holy Temple waits;
Destruction—death to all within its gates:⁴
Passing the pure and limpid fountain, where
David and Solomon did their Songs prepare;ᵛ
It reaches Pompey's camp; whose eagles lay,
Waiting his word to pounce upon their prey;
When they had soared in one triumphant feast;
And spread their wings in conquest o'er the East.ˣ

Through Gihon's vale the wall now takes its
course,
In lines direct, and with commens'rate force;
In front of Herod's palace now they build,
Where that arch tyrant cruelly had spilled
His kindred blood; here it was he slew
Queen Marianne, and her offspring too;ᶻ
'Twas here the Magi came at his command,
Trav'ling from far to seek the promised land,
Guided, by Heaven, to that same spot of earth—
Bethlehem—appointed for the Saviour's birth;

Whose streets with slaughtered Innocents were strewed,
To glut the vengeance of a monster shrewd;
One who in jealousy and cunning sought
The infant Jesus' life; who vainly thought
He had the power to stay th' Almighty's will,
While his vile deeds but prophecy fulfil."
'Twas in those sumptuous halls John Baptist's head,
Dissevered, bleeding, in a charger spread;
Another king, of self-same name and race,
Granted a wanton, who with matchless grace,
Had danced before him: taught by a mother's wiles,
She asks the gift from his approving smiles.ᵛ
Oh! tyrant princes! Oh! inhuman kings!
Is 't not enough the heathen with him brings
Battle and bonds?   Must ye surpass his wrong,
And add, by crimes atrocious, to the throng
Of woes, oppressions, danger and disgrace,
And raise God's wrath against this Holy place?

    Circumvallation now to make complete,
They draw their lines contiguous to the seat
Of that dire tragedy, that stampt the State
With Gentile ignorance and Jewish hate:
There, on that mount, the cross of Jesus stood—
Jesus the wise, the holy, and the good;
Two other crosses, one on either side,
Bore the transgressors who with Jesus died.
A band of soldiers, Pilate did despatch
To guard the pris'ners and the crowd to watch,

And at their head, the good Centurion who
Had seen His power—His healing mercy knew.
Priests, scribes and pharisees, the place attend,
Curious to mark His sufferings, and His end.
Some mocked, some prayed, some on His tortures
      railed ;
While other few, His lingering death bewailed :
Here knelt His weeping mother and her kin ;
There sat the soldiers with unholy grin,
Heedless of all things—eager but to win
His sacred vesture—when His garments, they
Had shared among them, in the face of day ;
Ere sudden darkness o'er the land prevailed ;
Earth shook, heaven vanish'd, and all nature quailed,
When in the midst of that tumultuous host,
His spirit fled, and He gave up the ghost.
Then that Centurion, in conviction cried,
"Truly the Son of God is crucified !"ʷ
Oh ! who can contemplate that awful scene,
Who can recall the mighty acts between
His birth and death ; and does not, must not see,
The will of God and Christ's humility,
Mercy divine and man's infirmity !

From this the site of Zion's crowning sin,
They join the camp from whence they did begin.

Within Jerusalem's walls what tongue can tell,
What mind can on her further miseries dwell !

Already does the siege destroy all hope,
'Tis vain, they know, with Roman arms to cope.
Yet do the Jews with desperate madness fight,
Hating each other, all the chiefs unite
To meet the fierce assault; all raise their cries
Against surrender, and all terms despise.
Fearful to view, within the city yet,
What crimes their animosities beget:
Murder and pillage, sacrilege and theft,
Absorb their souls—no fear, no pity left.
Like daemons now, these ruthless robbers run
Through streets and lanes—all ties of kindred shun;
Laugh when they stab, then mock their victim's
.   cry—
Extort his gold, and leave him there to die.
Beyond e'en death, their avarice impels
Their rage for plunder—crime itself excels!
Those who had hoped to 'scape the bloody strife
And save their treasure, dear to them as life,
Are disembowelled, ere their breath be sped,
Or ere their bodies numbered with the dead,
These cruel monsters, heedless of the gore,
Search in their entrails for the hidden store;
Groping with blood-stained fingers till they find
The jewelled trophies life has left behind.ˣ
Oh! matchless wickedness! Oh! cruel spite!
What beasts of prey, what vultures in their flight,
Could furnish forth such ravages as here
Man heaps on man, to crowd the funeral bier?

With evil passions nature now contends,
To the beleaguered town the Angel sends
Another scourge, to aggravate their ill:
Hunger and want their cup of misery fill.
No ingress now, no succour from without,
Famine, with hideous aspect stalks about,
Enters their dwellings, families destroys,
And with unheard-of crimes and horrors—cloys;
Subverts all order, nature's ties dissolves,
Tramples on reason and the brute evolves.
How human suffering did my mind excite!
What dreadful objects did my soul affright!
Swollen, ghastly, panting with unwholsome breath,
Reeling they fall, in agonies of death:
All unclean animals they kill for meat,
Then driven by hunger, human flesh they eat:
A mother here, her only offspring slays,
Then on its soddened flesh voracious preys:
Armed with a knife, her madden'd features glare,
Forbidding those to touch, who claim to share
In her inhuman feast: "My own! My own!"
She shrieks aloud, and scares them with her
      frown.[5]

Revolting scenes my soul in anguish bind,
My troubled spirit groans for human kind,
O'erwhelming terror thrills through every vein,
O'erpowering thoughts tumultuous crowd my brain;—
Instant—an unseen Power all thoughts denounced,
Instant—these words like thunder were pronounced,

" Ask not of God, nor question His decree,
" His will 's sufficient for mankind and thee :"
Trembling in all humility I cried,
" Lord, let thy will henceforward be my guide !"

Again my view was bent upon the spot
Where rage the foes, where most the battle's hot
Antonia's tower,—the fierce contested prize,
The Jews would hold it, but their fate denies :
By Titus' soldiers won,—the ruins lay,—
For his victorious arms, a broader way :
'Twas here these hands were first in duresse bound,
'Twas here the people 'compassed me around,
Making disturbance in the Temple court,
Where I, to pay my vows, had made resort :
Antonia's castle !—from whose stairs I spoke,
When from the multitude of Jews I broke ;
Who would have slain me there,—but Lysias came,
And saved me from their burning choler's flame ;
Borne by his soldiers, I escaped their ire,
Live to fulfil my destiny entire. ²

And now the Jews, encumbered with their dead,
Denied all egress, where the Romans tread ;
To other means of sepulture resort,
Some they enclose in houses,—some in sport
They cast remorseless o'er the outward wall ;
Shroudless, in death's deformity they fall,
To lay and putrefy by hundreds there,
While pestilential vapours fill the air. ³³

As Titus rides his customary rounds,
This awful sight the warrior's mind astounds;
His face is reared to Heaven,—his brow expands,—
Breathing this prayer, as stretching forth his hands:
" Oh! God of human kind! Jehovah! Jove!
" Ruler of kings! Omniscient Power above!
" Lay not this dreadful carnage to my charge,
" Withhold Thy judgments, and my heart enlarge,—
" Set free,—from crimes my spirit does detest,
" And let Thy vengeance on their leaders rest:
" Bear witness with me, I have sought all schemes
" To soothe their hatred, and convert their dreams,
" Of war and death,—to tranquilness and peace:
" Of this fatality my soul release." [bb]

With this the chief on speedy action bent,
Quits the sad scene, and rides towards his tent;
As if some new-born thought now strikes his soul,
To seize, prevent, or circumvent the whole;
There he dismounts, and calls a council round,
To weigh, consult, consider well the ground
Of some new master-stroke, the war to end,
And to the Roman yoke the rebels bend.

From three strong outworks in succession driven,
Not without proofs of equal vengeance given,
(For wounded in his tent Nicanor lies,
Josephus powerless from his couch to rise,) [cc]
Not without fierce encounters on the wall,
Where none ask quarter, none for mercy call,

The Jews not vanquished yet, in force dispute
The foe's advance, and yield but foot by foot;
Till Roman skill and discipline combined,
Force them to flee, until they refuge find,
Within the Temple's courts, and sad to tell
God's Holy House they make a citadel:
With clanging arms her pavement now resounds,
With blood-stained men her cloister now abounds,
Of purest worship once the chosen seat,
Now the rebellious army's last retreat. [dd]

The assembled council Titus now dissolves,
With their assent united, he resolves
To storm the Temple,—wrench it with his bands,
From Jewish grasp and sacrilegious hands,
Restore her ancient worship, that she may
Remain a monument of Roman sway.

At night the Roman cohorts are arrayed,
Leaders appointed,—dispositions made,
To scale the outward wall, her gates assail
And o'er the Jews in conquest to prevail.
Titus commanding, from a tower above,
Surveys them all, and gives the word to move:
" Advance Tiberius; Sextus—thou advance;[ee]
" Destroy these murderers,—give them not a chance
" War to prolong;—be this the final blow,
" Rome to exalt, and lay their nation low:
" On! fellow soldiers,—cherish your renown,
" Make sure your conquest,—win the mural crown;"

He spake, with Berenicé by his side,
Who to the chieftains, thus imploring cried,—
" Oh ! spare the Temple, our sanctuary spare ;
" War not with God, whose instruments ye are,
" But chase, disperse, these traitors from her courts,
" Whose arms profane,—nor heaven nor earth sup-
      ports." "

With firm and measured step the wall they reach
In one strong phalanx,—first to make a breach,
They with their wonted energy apply
Their battering rams ;—more daring others try
With scaling ladders, entrance to obtain,
And on the wall unequal fight maintain :
Standing to meet the bold aspiring foe,
The Jews the upward climbers overthrow,
And hurl the assailants backward on the ground ;
Headlong they tumble—pierced with many a wound :
Exulting o'er their victims as they fall,
Thus to their foes the Jews reviling call,
" 'Thou'dst come to Jerusalem,—would'st thou ?—
      come—
" And be Jerusalem thy final home." "

Titus, indignant that his men retired,
Commands, and instantly the gates are fired ;
In rush the legions,—now the Jews recede,
Fighting they fly,—at every pore they bleed,—
Vengeance pursues,—no pity, no remorse :
Despair alone now arms them with a force

K

Beyond themselves ;—their spirit unsubdued,
Reeking with blood, all fear of death eschewed,
They turn again,—the murd'rous fight restore,
And dye the Temple's floor and sides with gore ;
That Holy Place, where Jesus healed and taught,
Where His disciples truth and wisdom sought,
Where in divine benignity He stood,
Is now the scene of massacre and blood :
In every court,—in every corner where
Arm can reach arm,—the flash of swords is there :—
No place too sacred—none too secret is ;
Satan now rules,—this day of triumph his :
The altar e'en, where hallowed victims bled,
With dead and dying men is now o'erspread ;
Romans and Jews, here intermingled lie ;
Victors and vanquish'd—hecatombs supply,
To mock the sacrifice of days gone by. [hh]

As stormy waves among the breakers hiss,
Lashing the rocks from out their dark abyss,
Foaming with rage,—surge dashing over surge :—
So human passions lash the heart ;—now urge
To some new feat all others should surpass,
And in one boiling whirlpool sink the mass :—
Eager for spoil, and madden'd with the strife,
A Roman soldier, warring to the knife,
Armed with a torch, commanding others' aid,—
Mounts to the window that 's with gold inlaid,—
Ignites the galleries, and parts about
The Holy House :—one loud, one general shout,

Proclaims the deed ;—no thunder from on high,
Can e'er exceed that one terrific cry :
Some turn and flee,—others their throats present
To Roman swords, their misery to prevent :—
Some with their destiny no longer strive,
Determined not their Temple to survive,—
In their own breasts the dagger's point they sheathe,
And on the Temple's floor, they cease to breathe."

Titus fatigued,—reclining in his tent,
Roused by the clamour that the air had rent,
Snatches his arms and hastens to the spot,
Where tumult reigns and discipline 's forgot :—
Sudden he halts,—is smitten with the sight,—
The Temple burning, and the Jews in flight :
Pride moves his heart, the citadel to take,—
The Temple spare, for Berenicé's sake : [jj]
Confusion round him—" Fronto," he exclaims,
" Hold back the soldiers—and subdue the flames !"—
Alas ! his words unheeded pass away ;
Order has fled,—revenge alone has sway :—
" Oh! save the Temple—save——!" his voice is drowned.
In din of arms, and fury that has crowned
The war's success :—the fire, the blaze ascends :
In vain his hand with gesture he extends,—
In vain commands Centurions to beat—
Prevent the soldiers :—signals to entreat—
Enforce obedience, are alike despised ;
Vengeance and plunder, before all are prized :

Nor love for him—nor fear of his reproof,
Availeth aught ;—allegiance they throw off :
At his commands and prayers alike they scoff. [kk]

To quell their fury he at length despairs,
Now with his chosen Captains he repairs,
To that once Holy Place, where none before,
Had dared to come, its secrets to explore ;
Pompey alone, of all the Roman lords, [ll]
Witnessed the sanctity its name affords :—
" Holy of Holies !" what religious awe,
Caus'd him to gaze, to wonder and withdraw ?
An unseen Power then touched his darkened soul,
An unknown God did all his thoughts control :
And Titus now with equal wonder views,
Its solemn amplitude, its form, its hues,
Its fair proportions, and its rich contents :
This he would save,—but force or fire prevents :
A higher Power his efforts render vain,
The fire to quench,—his soldiers to restrain ;
The Angel of Destruction hovers o'er,
And seals the Temple's doom for evermore. [mm]

END OF THE FIFTH BOOK.

NOTES TO BOOK V.

^a Page 112. The historian has been more than commonly minute in unknowingly recording the fulfilment of the sublimely pathetic prophecy of Our Lord (Luke xix. 41) in regard to the desolation of Jerusalem, for he even gives the name of the Roman—Terentius Rufus—left in command by Titus, and commissioned by him to plough up Sion as a field.—*Josephus*, Book vii. ch. 11.

^b Page 113. The amazing amount of treasure—two thousand talents (equal to £1,296,000 sterling of our money)—together with the golden candlestick and table, and other utensils of Jewish worship all made entirely of gold, and (although more than a century had elapsed since Pompey left them untouched) would be likely to raise the army's hopes and expectations.

^c Page 113. The loves of Titus and Berenicé have been the subject of dramatic poetry. One of the Corneilles and Racine each wrote a play about it, which are still, I believe, extant in the original, though it has never been my chance to fall in with them. The marriage of the son of the Emperor with a foreign princess, and she a Jewess, whose nation was never very highly prized by the Romans, would not be conformable to Roman law or custom; but as the Evangelist in the Acts of the Apostles (xxvi. 24) calls Drusilla the *wife* of Felix, we may rationally conclude that Berenicé was the wife of Titus, and that she lived with him as such in the East; but on their arrival at Rome, he found popular prejudice so much against the match that he was compelled to repudiate her, and they separated with mutual reluctance and grief. This part of Tacitus' history has not come down to us, therefore must we chiefly depend on Suetonius *c.* Titus.

^d Page 113. Acts of the Apostles, xxvi. 30.

e Page 114. Antiochus; the fourth King of Syria of that name. He was surnamed Epiphanes, but called by the Jews " Epimanes," or the " Furious," in consequence of his cruel treatment of their nation, as related by Josephus both in his *Antiquities* and his *History of the Wars.*

f Page 115. Pompey's treatment of the Jews, after he had taken Jerusalem and added the whole of Palestine and Syria to the Roman territories, was that of a humane conqueror, who respected their religious ceremonies and sanctioned their worship.

g Page 116. The ambush formed by the Jews, to surprise and intercept Titus when reconnoitering their city unarmed, and accompanied only by a small guard, is strictly historical.—*Josephus*, Book v., ch. 11, sec. 2.

h Page 117. The providential preservation of Titus in this skirmish must have appeared to the pious mind of Josephus nothing less than a miraculous interposition of the Almighty.

i Page 117. The rebuilding, improving, and adorning the Temple, was the munificent act of Herod the Great; and the fame of its beauty and magnificence had spread throughout the East, and had also reached Rome.

j Page 117. St. Luke's Gospel, xxi. 21.

k Page 118. The fact of the site of the judgment of the Almighty visited upon the Assyrians, as related in Isaiah xxxvii., also 2 Kings xix., remaining known after a lapse of 780 years, is in no small degree corroborative of the truth of Scripture.

l Page 118. The stratagems and treachery of the Jews during the siege are minutely recorded by Josephus in his *History.*

m Page 119. Crucifixion was a Roman punishment which they had learnt or copied from the Carthaginians, and had been inflicted by their Governors or Procurators on the Jews, whether malefactors, or rebels against their authority. During the siege by Titus, there were so many that suffered this punishment that there was scarce room for the crosses to stand or wood to make them. Among them all, there must have been some who had witnessed the execution on Mount Calvary, as hardly a generation had passed away since that awful day.

n Page 119. The frequent overtures that Josephus made to his countrymen on his own account, out of the love he had for his country and his regard for the Holy House as well as the commands of Titus, only increased their hatred and contempt of one whom they considered a renegade from their cause and faith.

" Page 120. The line of circumvallation which Titus drew round the walls of Jerusalem, and thereby " kept them in on every side," must have passed over or near to the site of many of the most prominent incidents in the life of Our Saviour during His sojourn on earth, as recorded in the New Testament, some of which are here particularized, and the lines attempted to be traced with as much accuracy as ancient records and the description of modern travellers will allow.

" Page 120.   St. Luke's Gospel, xxiv. 13—34.

" Page 121.   St. Luke's Gospel, xiii. 4.

" Page 121.   This relic of antiquity is still preserved entire, and according to tourists is frequented by Arab women, who descend the worn steps to fill their pitchers from the fountain, by the side of which David and Solomon, it is supposed, composed their holy Songs.

" Page 121.   The site of Pompey's camp is not so easily identified as that of the Assyrians, though it is near 700 years later ; according to the old maps it lay opposite the south-west corner of the city.

" Page 121.   Josephus' *Antiquities*, Book xv. ch. 7.

" Page 122.   St. Matthew's Gospel, ii. 16, 17, 18.

" Page 122.   St. Matthew's Gospel, xiv. 1—13.

" Page 123.   St. Matthew xxvii. ; St. Mark xv. ; St. Luke xxiii. ; St. John xix.

" Page 124.   This most cruel and atrocious practice was commenced by the Jews themselves, and quickly adopted by the Roman auxiliary soldiers, whose greedy desire of plunder Titus could not restrain, though he punished several of the perpetrators with death.

" Page 125.   Josephus' *Wars*, Book vi. ch. 2.

" Page 126.   Acts of the Apostles, xxi. 30, to the end ; also xxiii. 10.   The castle or tower of Antonia, so named after a daughter of Mark Antony, Herod's patron, was joined on to the north-west corner of the Temple, and was ascended by stone steps, which commanded a full view of the cloisters, from which steps or stairs St. Paul spoke to the Jews

[a] Page 126. *Josephus,* Book v. ch. 9.

[bb] Page 127. Titus, from his friendly intercourse with Josephus and his connubial intimacy with Berenicé, must have had a perfect knowledge of their creed; and it is not improbable that he should have invoked their Deity by name, when he witnessed such a dreadful instance of His vengeance.

[cc] Page 127. These two eminent warriors had both been wounded during the siege, as related by Josephus himself, Book v., ch. xiii. 3; *Nicanor,* Book iv., ch. vi. 2.

[dd] Page 128. The strength of the Temple as a fortification, and the blind infatuation or invincible obstinacy of the Jews, caused them to cling to the hope that the Deity would yet preserve the Holy House from the profane hands of the heathen soldiers, though they themselves were defiling it with blood.

[ee] Page 128. Tiberius Alexander, second in command of the whole army, and Sextus Cerealis, the commander of the Fifth Legion, with Fronto, another leader of importance, were the three whom Titus particularly addressed.—*Josephus,* Book vi., ch. vi. see. 2, 3.

[ff] Page 129. It is natural to suppose that Berenicé, a Jewess, and a descendant of Herod the Great, would be most anxious to save the Temple from destruction.

[gg] Page 129. It has been related, that at the siege of Badajoz—one of the most arduous, the most difficult, and therefore the most brilliant of our great commander's achievements in the Peninsular War—a French soldier on the parapet, at the appearance of the foremost assailant, thrust him back with his bayonet, and in his fall coolly called out to him, "Ah! vous voulez entrer dans Badajoz? Eh bien! entrez donc!" In a similar way would the Jews taunt the Romans when repulsing their first assault.

[hh] Page 130. The slaughter of the Jews here must have been enormous, as many chose to die upon the altar and on the spot where their ancestors had offered so many sacrifices.

[ii] Page 131. Their Temple in flames, the Jews thought all further resistance vain, and therefore sought a voluntary death.

ij Page 131. However Titus in his clemency might have wished to spare the Temple, or the innermost part of it, there can be little doubt but he was influenced by his regard for Berenicé, which stimulated him to endeavour to prevent its complete destruction by those exertions recorded in *Josephus*, Book v. ch. 4.

kk Page 132. The Roman history is rife with the devotion displayed by the legioniares to their commanders; but in this instance the love of vengeance and plunder surpassed all other passions in intensity and force.

ll Page 132. The sanctity of the Holy of Holies had been respected by Augustus Cæsar and his successors, with the exception of Caligula, whose attempt to defile it, however, proved abortive.

mm Page 132. Thus was the Temple destroyed by the will of God, according to the historian, and its desolation remains a fulfilment of prophecy.

BOOK VI.

—

THE VISION

CONTINUED.

THE PERSECUTION OF THE CHRISTIANS; OR, CONSTANTINE THE GREAT.

——◆——

ARGUMENT.

PAUL continues his narration. The dispersion of the Jews. Vain attempt of the Emperor Julian to recall them and rebuild their Temple—The truth of Prophecy as exemplified thereby—The spreading of the Gospel compared to the growth of the vine—Proof against every hindrance. Paul's and his followers' approaching sufferings and death only a forerunner of others equally cruel and tyrannical. Persecution obtains first in the Eastern provinces—The martyrdom of St. Ignatius—is dragged in chains from Antioch to Rome—is thrown to the wild beasts in the Amphitheatre—Paul's comments on his devoted courage and constancy. Carthage. The martyrdom of St. Cyprian—is brought before the Proconsul—is commanded to burn incense to their gods—upon his refusal is condemned to death — is beheaded amidst a concourse of people, who bewail his loss. The noble conduct of the primitive Christians. The persecution in Gaul and Spain—Britain hitherto free from it—The happy position of the island—its fecundity and future destiny. The Gospel not destroyed, but strengthened, under successive persecutions. The last and worst under Diocletian—its enormities—Constantius Chlorus in Britain. Boadicea.—The martyrdom of St. Alban—shelters a Christian Priest at Verulam—causes his escape from his pursuers—presents himself to the soldiers dressed in the Priest's raiment — is taken before the

Prætor—confesses himself a Christian—denounces the heathen gods
—is sentenced to be first scourged and then beheaded—is drawn to
the place of execution, and on his way converts his executioner.
Constantine succeeds his father Constantius Chlorus, and is invested
with the Imperial Purple at York—Protects the followers of Christ—
His person and character—Embarks for Gaul—Crosses the Alps—
His rapid and continued successes in Italy—Encamps his army before
the city—His appearance under the influence of a dream—His conversion—Consecrates a new standard to Christ—His soldiers assume
the Cross. Battle of the Milvian Bridge—The miraculous Vision—
Defeat and death of Maxentius — Constantine enters Rome—The
Church triumphant.

THE PERSECUTION OF THE CHRISTIANS; OR,
CONSTANTINE THE GREAT.

———◆——

Thus falls our Holy House—then fails to live
The Jewish nation—for the Romans give
No hope of restoration to the State,
No rise from her irrevocable fate :
In vain against the Cæsars they rebel,
Their kindly acts despitefully repel ;
And seek by strife and bloodshed to reclaim
A glorious future and their former fame ;
As well the shackled slave may ceaseless strive
To burst his bonds, as they their rule revive :
Age follows age, and kings succeed to kings,
But the long roll of time no future brings ;
Her ancient splendour is for ever gone,
God's favour cancelled, and her race undone ;
Scatter'd throughout the earth in every clime,
Their name a bye-word and their creed a crime.
One out of all the many ruling powers,
Fain would recall them and rebuild their towers :
Vain are his efforts—so his power is vain,
The heathen's falling temples to sustain.
Apostate to the truth—a madman he,
Who would subvert the Mighty One's decree."

Then did I see those mournful words fulfilled,
That Jesus sorrowing spake, when grief distilled
Tears from those eyes that never wept on earth,
Save when or love or pity gave them birth: [b]
Deploring Zion's fate, His tongue foretold
The direful judgment that I now unfold:
Who can deny His truth—dispute His word?—
When, through the course of ages has occurred
So sure a test—so manifest a sign,
Of rule omnipotent—prescience Divine?
So will it be to ages yet unborn,
To all but those philosophers who scorn
Such revelations as from Heaven are shewn,
And seek no knowledge higher than their own—
Who look to nature's laws, and not to One,
That governs nature, and is God alone.

Then was it given me to mark the growth
('Midst Jews' antipathy, and Gentiles loth
To see, and comprehend the truth divine,)
Of this our infant but enduring vine:
What though the tyrant threatens to uproot
Its tender fibrils—tear away each shoot!
Our death shall but his madden'd vengeance mock:
What though the cross, the lion, and the block
Torture our frames!—still shall our blood remain,
The roots to nurture and the plant maintain.

Through what variety of clime and race,
Could I its strong and sinuous branches trace;

Extending now throughout the Roman world,
Its growth establish'd, and its leaves unfurl'd,
Displays the opening blossom, and defies
The blights that oft from heathen hate arise :
Worldly philosophy—despotic power,
Unite to crush—destroy, the heavenly flower ;
Trodden by force—elastic it regains
Its pristine vigour, and its strength retains. ^c

But in the vista of revolving years,
What blood-stain'd scene before mine eyes appears !
Our immolation, alas ! is but the first, ^d
Offered on altars of their gods accursed ;
Repeated oft, by tyrants such as this,
Who seek by death and terror to dismiss
The Gospel light, from out their widened realm—
A light that shall their worship overwhelm.
In every Province I can well descry
The fate of hundreds, who for Jesus die :
First in those cities famed throughout the East,
Ephesus, Smyrna, Tarsus not the least, ^e
I see the victims of our holy creed,
With courage suffer, and in torture bleed.

Egypt and Syria, both attest the truth ;—
In plain and city—age and blushing youth,
Of either sex, attend the judgment-seat,
And from their rulers eagerly entreat
That crown of martyrdom that we must wear,
Our fate to rival and our glory share. ^f

Guarded by soldiers, dragged in chains along,
Through Antioch's streets, where men and women throng
To catch a parting blessing from their chief,
An aged Bishop—who, in counsel brief,
Exhorts them to be stedfast, and adhere
To Jesus' standard—banish every fear:
To this Imperial city he is sent
Condemn'd to torture—have his body rent
By savage animals from distant climes,
Whose thirst for blood with heathen owners chimes:
The Amphitheatre—the chosen place,
Wherein assemble some of every race
And either sex, but all devoid of grace,
To mark his end—his cruel death to trace:
With what a lowly, yet determined mien,
He views the crowd advancing to the screen,
His front unruffled,—his beseeching eye,
Invites them all to see a Christian die;
Then turning to the stage—upon his knees
In fervent prayer, he scarce the lion sees;
No sign of fear—no trepidation mars
His resolution, or his spirit jars:
The beast approaching, glances on his prey,—
Then sudden turns contemptuously away,
As if such conquest were beneath his ire,
And fiercer game his tendencies require:
A second then, and then a third they loose—
They, their appointed food likewise refuse:
Uprising then, he urges them to fight,
Provokes their anger—puts forth all his might,

With kicks and blows to stimulate their rage,
And make them in their human feast engage :
Surprised, the people shout—the slaves apply
Hot burning spears, their savage mood to try ;
But fruitless all,—unmindful of the cry,
Close at his feet the crouching lions lie.

Like some frail, fluttering insect, in the hands
Of babes and innocents, unhurt he stands :
Courting, not fearing death, he seems a king
That conquers terrors and the tyrant's sting :
Amazed, the crowd, impatient of delay,
Call for more beasts, to finish the affray :
Two tigers now are launched upon the stage,
Roaring and bristling with unbridled rage ;
Furious, voracious, on their prey they glare ;
The motley multitude 'cry out and stare,'
As at a bound they seize him with their claws,
And grasp his body with distended jaws :
No groan escapes him ; soon his life is void,—
Piecemeal devoured,—his frame is soon destroyed :
Loud acclamations from the crowd arise,
As the wild beasts tear, limb from limb, their prize :
Besmeared with blood, they pace the circus round,
His riven bones lay scattered on the ground.

Behold, ye nations—see what man can dare
When armed with faith that Christians only share ;
The tyrant's power triumphant he defies ;
Death claims his own,—his spirit upward flies.

L.

Earth his example ever must regard—
Heaven will his truth and constancy reward. *

    Then were mine eyes attracted to the coast
Where Carthage stands, of Africa the boast :
Renowned for arms and enterprise of yore,
For labourers now in Christian vineyards more ;
Warriors and chiefs her ancient scroll engage—
Soldiers of Christ will grace her future page :
For persecution now her arm extends—
To the Imperial edicts Afric bends :
In her famed city many champions dwell,
Who now are called upon her list to swell
With one, whose faith and zeal surpasses most :
Fronting the Roman judges, they accost—
Accuse him first, as leader of the sect
Who treat their fathers' worship with neglect,
Insult their gods, profess another creed,
From ancient forms and ceremonies freed ;
Command him, then, from this new faith to turn,
And on their heathen altars incense burn :—
Calm he refuses,—confident he pleads
His sacred office, that devotion needs :
No further witness,—instantly condemned,—
His followers' tears and threats alike contemned,
They marshal him without the city gates,
Where crowds assemble, and where death awaits :
His faithful friends attend him to the plain,
While tribunes and centurions guard the train ;

Without disturbance, and with brow serene,
His fate he ponders, and surveys the scene:
A solemn silence all the host pervades,
No Gentile taunts him, and no Jew upbraids:
With modest look he patiently disrobes,
Master of every thought that sometimes probes
The human heart, when dissolution's near,
His spirit's buoyant, and he knows no fear:
God gives him courage to sustain the shock,
Kneeling, he lays his head upon the block;
And, as the soldier lifts his arm on high,
From out the throng, one deep convulsive sigh,
Follows the blow that separates his head,
And lays him numbered with the holy dead;—
At night his corpse they bear with tears away,
With care consign it to its kindred clay.

Thus do Christ's soldiers nobly act their parts,—
No fear of death afflicts His followers' hearts—
No punishment strikes terror to their souls,
When immortality their thoughts controuls;
Prayers and thanksgivings to their God arise,
When faith in Him demands life's sacrifice. [h]

From this my face turned to the opposing shore,
Where Gaul and Spain their destiny deplore;
Here too the tide of persecution flows—
Here, where the Gospel's taken root and grows;
The o'erwhelming flood—the same malignant power,
Threatens to swamp and deluge every bower;

To stop the rushing waters—stay the tide—
What courage, strength, and constancy are tried!
But firm their faith, and all will not prevail,
However death and torture may assail ;
Victims are found to quell the foaming wave,
The direful tempest's utmost fury brave. [i]

In distant Britain what do I perceive!—
Here, in this favoured land, no tyrants grieve,--
Affright the soul, with threats of pain and death,
No Christians here, in tremor draw their breath ;
For here in safety they preserve their faith,
Worship their God, and have no foe to scathe :
As in this island savage beasts ne'er tread,
Or noxious reptiles 'round their poison spread,
So in the human form, from monsters free,
They live secure—nor distant dangers see. [j]

Thou blest abode !—The suffering sinner's choice!
How does thine aspect make my soul rejoice !
Thy clime so tempered, and thy soil so kind,
That nature's choicest gifts are here combined :
Oh ! fruitful isle, where vine and olive thrive,
And golden cereals annually revive ;
Where the green pastures teem with lowing herds,
And shady groves abound with warbling birds ;
Where fleecy flocks ascend the mountain's side,
While her fixed base repels the ocean's tide ;—
That ocean's limits, destined to survey,
O'er all her regions bear a sovereign sway,—

Extend our faith—of future rule the seat!—
But now of poor believers the retreat. ᵏ

    Thus generations pass in turn away,
Alternate peace and hideous war have sway ;
Yet does the Gospel suffer no decay,—
Flourishes still, and brightens with its ray :
As fleeting clouds obscure the moon's pale face,
When they across the sky each other chase ;
No sooner from the one escapes her orb,
Than others seem her beauty to absorb ;
So to destroy our creed, these tyrants vie
In cruel edicts—then in turn they die ;
Leaving a pure but intermittent light,
Shining the brighter in a stormy night.

    Another threatening tempest I descry,
A blacken'd cloud that fills the Roman sky ;
A deeper, deadlier shade, it now presents,
Then on the earth its fiercest fury vents :
From out its darkness, persecution's darts,
Like lightning strikes and penetrates all parts ;
From Nicomedia issues the decree,
Announcing death, destruction, enmity,
To all that to the Christian faith belong :
Churches demolished,—sanctuaries strong,
Where numbers meet to worship in His name,
Become the victims of one mighty flame :
Nor fire alone, but every torture tried,
With devilish ingenuity applied,

To shake their constancy—from mercy free;—
When all has failed,—they cast them in the sea.[1]

While my heart sickens at this fearful sight,
From out the cloud's extremity a light,
As of the morning star, shines mildly forth,
Emblem of Truth ascending in the North:—
A star it seems,—the harbinger of one,
Whose greater lustre, like the noon-day sun,
Shall pierce the darkness—dissipate the cloud,
Revive the timid, and subdue the proud:
It rises now o'er distant Britain's isle;
A chief rules there by nature free from guile,
Who scorns the weapons that the tyrants wield,
And guards the faith with his unsullied shield;
But not before a Christian hero dies,—
First in this land to fall a sacrifice.[m]

'Twas on the spot, where late the Icenian Queen
Harangued her army,—pointing to the scene,
Where lay the foe, behind intrenchments hid,
Whose flight, she urged, their vengeance must forbid;
Vengeance for stripes inhumanly bestowed,—
Her daughter's injuries, a vengeful load,—
Vengeance for insult, cruelty and crime,
They and their fathers suffer'd, from the time
The Roman galleys touched their sea-girt shore,
And British kings the badge of slavery wore:
This was the day their valour to maintain,—
This was the day their freedom to regain;

Alas! that day how many thousands slain!
How blood of Britons deluged all the plain!
Defeated, vanquished, not again disgraced ;—
The Queen a voluntary death embraced:
Unhappy people! destined to become
The first of nations,—now the slaves of Rome. "

A Christian soldier dies upon this spot,
Whose pure devotion ne'er will be forgot :
In Verulamium's city I forsee,
Disciples who from persecution flee ;
A preacher one—a servant of the Lord,
Who comes to propagate His holy word,
'Mongst heathen soldiers, fearing not at all
That on his head their vengeance he should call :
His hated doctrines and his speech provoke
Their rancorous anger ; from their rage he broke,
And seeks his safety in a speedy flight ;
Swift they pursue him—he eludes their sight,—
Reaches the dwelling of a Roman knight,—
Claims his protection—instant peril shows ;—
The knight admits him, and—the portals close.
In that one act, the sheltered guest perceives
The noble nature of his host, and grieves
That such a mind should own a pagan's soul ;
Then without preface, hindrance or controul,
He preaches Jesus ; silent and aghast,
The astonished knight at once conceives the vast—
The comprehensive attributes of God :
Scorning the creed in which his youth had trod :

Long disinclined in error to persist,
His wise monitions he could not resist ;
But earnestly implores his stranger guest,
To pour the truthful knowledge in his breast :
Humble in spirit, and subdued in thought,
He hears with gladness all the preacher taught ;
Becomes a convert to his holy creed,
Willing to die for Jesus' sake, if need :—
That need 's at hand—for voices at the gate
Call for admission;—soon the preacher's fate
With apprehension fills the Roman's mind,
Knowing from them no mercy he will find :
With what satanic zeal they trace his route !
With what vindictive spleen they search him out !
While with devoted love he hastes to save
The holy man—their utmost malice brave !
For his escape the two their plans arrange,—
First their distinctive garments they exchange,—
Then seek the postern—kneeling on the floor,—
One fervent prayer—they part to meet no more.

Meantime, the crowd assembled round the hall
Renew their clamour,—for his presence call :
In the delinquent's garb the knight appears,
Mild is his aspect—unclouded as he rears
His brow determined,—eyes them at a glance,—
Demands their office,—bids them all advance :
They seek the Christian priest—surprised they see,
Their fellow-soldier, robed,—disguised as he :

To seize their prisoner, they abashed refrain ;
Then were these words impress'd upon my brain :
" Nay, start not, brethren !—lead me to our chief ;
" To his tribunal let our march be brief ! "
Silent, with folded arms he walks along,—
So strange an object, 'midst an escort strong,
Attracts the notice of the gazing throng,
Who follow to the Forum, where in state
The Prætor with his armed council wait :
Undaunted he, before his judges stands,—
Raising his head and spreading out his hands ;
He openly declares himself the priest,—
The Christian priest—not worthy in the least
To be compared to him whose blood they sought,
Whose safety he with his own life had bought ;
A convert to the truth,—by mercy made,—
They would not have Christ's messenger betrayed :
Christian he is—and Christians abjure all
Those dæmons vile, ' whom gods they falsely call : '
" Enough ! enough ! " I hear them loudly cry ;
" This man is guilty—he must surely die ;
" But first, ye lictors, scourge him with your rods,
" That he may feel the vengeance of our gods ;
" Then with the headsman, take him to the hill,
" Facing the gates—his sentence there fulfil. "

To act their part the lictors now prepare ;
Doft his assumed garb—his back laid bare—
The rods applied,—blood flows from every stroke ;—
No repetition does his ire provoke :

Unflinching, he the punishment receives,—
No sigh or groan—but for his torturer grieves :
Unmoved they place him bleeding in a wain,
To bear him up the steep, six oxen strain ;
Close by his side the executioner sits,
To whom his faith he earnestly transmits :
First admiration strikes the heathen's heart,
Compassion then, and sorrow, do their part ;
And as they reach the height, he stands confessed
A brother Christian—with this deed oppressed :
Trembling, the fatal instrument he holds,
The knight observes, and thus his will unfolds—
" If to the one true God thy thoughts incline,
" Of thy conversion this shall be the sign ;
" Mine orders thou wert 'customed to obey,
" Now do the Lord's, and let His word have sway ;
" If severed at a blow, my head roll off,
" Thy faith's established—thou hast done enough."
Thus re-assured, the man performs his task,
His prayers ascend to Heaven and pardon ask.

On this famed spot, in distant times I see
A spacious Temple reared, that long shall be
A monument of glory to the Saint,
Whose pure and fervent faith knew no constraint. °

Now from his golden bed the rising sun
Dims the bright star that had his course forerun ;
Ascends the heavens—his majesty displays—
And cheers the heart with his resplendent rays ;

Meridian lustre 'round the Gospel shines,
His genial warmth our holy faith entwines,—
Preserves its followers from all earthly strife,
Promotes its doctrines, and imparts new life.
In Ebor's city now arises one,
Who in succession mounts his father's throne ;
That father's love for Christian rites he shares,—
That father's last injunctions he declares,
Shall be his rule towards the injured sect,
Resolved their faith from insult to protect :
His lofty stature, his majestic mien,
Graceful deportment, and his front serene,
Wins the esteem of all the standers by,
While burns his soul with aspirations high ;
A warrior brave,—a chief with skill endowed,—
Justice his aim,—of power and wisdom proud,
He walks the earth like some superior lord,
A master-mind in every look and word. ᴾ

In Gallia's regions first his strength he tries,
To Heaven he looks—on God's support relies,
As he surveys the galleys' crowded decks,
And on his future destiny reflects :
God's instrument he is—by Him design'd
To raise the Gospel in the people's mind :
Ardent with hope he quits his father's land,—
Bristling with arms the galleys reach the strand ;
At his approach the affrighted heathens fly,—
Both treacherous friends and angry foemen die :

With matchless prudence he reforms the State,
Exalts the humble and restrains the great,—
Enacts new laws—protects the Church, and leaves
In peace his Province ; while his arm retrieves
The fallen fortunes of unhappy Rome,
Writhing beneath a ruthless tyrant's doom. [4]

The snow-clad summits of the Alps he gains,
Now pours his legions on Italia's plains ;
His warlike genius soars o'er every field,
To his courageous army all must yield ;—
Town after town he rapidly subdues ;
Chief after chief successful he pursues ;
Leads his victorious arms to Tiber's banks,
Where veteran legions in extended ranks,
Arrest his progress—stop his onward march,—
Dispute his passing Rome's triumphal arch ;—
Intrenched, his camp he forms upon a ridge,
Fronting the city—near the Milvian bridge :
When from the foe's attack his men he shields,
His wearied body to repose he yields.

As in sleep's soft oblivion he is lost,
What pleasing visions and what dreams accost ;
Like the Archangel upon earth he seems,
Favour Divine in every feature gleams ;
His lips apart—some impress he receives,—
His breast instinctively with impulse heaves ;
As if some holy messenger had come,
To bring him tidings of the morrow's doom,—

Some new-born spirit animates his frame,
His glowing cheeks some heavenly gift proclaim :—
Still wrapt in sleep, he holds his arm on high,
Seeming to grasp some object in the sky ;—
Then firmly holds it—clasps it to his heart,
Resolved from thence it never shall depart :—
No pains oppress him, no convulsive throes,
His bold aspiring spirit undergoes ;
Armed though he be, his pillow angels smooth—
Angels his cares with peaceful slumber soothe. ^r

   Conscious he 'wakes—refreshed in soul and frame,
And on the Son of God he calls by name,—
Acknowledges His truth—believes His word,—
Invokes His aid—devotes to Him his sword ;—
Declares himself the champion of His cause,
Resolves to govern by His gospel's laws :
In Jesus' name he rears a Standard new,
Pledge of his faith—to his Redeemer due ;
A banner consecrates to God most true,
Commits its safety to the charge of few,
Renowned for force, fidelity and truth,--
Men born in Christ—companions from their youth
In all his battles—men who value more
Their faith and duty than aught else before ;
Their faith in Christ—whose soldiers they are now,
To keep the Standard in His name they vow :
The army marshall'd on the embattled field,
The Cross of Christ emblazons every shield ;

On every helm the Christian symbol's worn;
As through the lines the sacred Standard's borne,
Each soldier signs the Cross upon his brow,—
All ranks behold it, and with reverence bow. *

Mounted,—the chief, in front of all the host,
Points with his sword to where the foe had cross'd
The deep and troubled river, that surrounds
Rome's heathen temples and her palace grounds;—
Where stands the tyrant's army in array,
Himself determined to dispute the day:
His veteran legions and prætorian guards,
Men who had shared his vices and rewards,
Flanked with Italian and Numidian horse,
Present a strong and formidable force:
The word is given the onslaught to prepare,—
Sudden—the earth's illumined with a glare,—
A light 'above the brightness of the sun'
Shines round about them, ere the fight's begun:
Smiting both chief and army with surprise,—
To Heaven they cannot, dare not, lift their eyes;
But raise their shields, their dazzled sight to screen,—
In silence ask what should this portent mean; '
Resembling that which near Damascus, I
Beheld with terror as it filled the sky,—
Struck my companions to the earth, and me,
Encircling all in one bright canopy;
This—like a brilliant meteor passes on,
Leaving a cloud for them to gaze upon;—

A cloud, still luminous, assumes the form
Of one stupendous Cross :—raising his arm,
And pointing to its figure in the sky,
" Conquer by this !"—I hear the chieftain cry ;
Now waves his sword and leads his army on,
One furious onset bears the foemen down :
Broken, dispersed, the horse defeated fly,—
Determined valour now the legions try.

In conflict dire, contending armies stand,—
This forms the Heathen—that the Christian band ;
With desperate madness, long the Heathen fight,
No hope of life, no safety in their flight ;—
In vain for succour on their gods they call,—
Vain strength and courage—fighting—there, they fall :
Faith arms the Christian with superior power ;
While on their enemies' heads their blows they shower,
The chief advances with the chosen band,
Bearing the sacred banner in their hand ;—
At one intrepid charge the foe's o'erthrown,—
The battle ended, and the field his own.

To reach the City now the vanquished try,
Fear lends them wings,—their pursuers nigh,—
Headlong they plunge into the rapid flood,
Flying and wounded dye the stream with blood :
Others attempt the Milvian bridge to pass,—
And here the tyrant, hurried by the mass
Of fear-struck fugitives, is swept along,—
Forced o'er the bridge,—and perishes among

The people's curses :—in the Tiber drowned,—
A Prince for crime and cruelty renowned. "

    The victor enters—the Flaminian way
Opes her wide gates, admits the proud array ;—
Onward they pass,—while Rome, without alloy,
Hails her deliverer with tumultuous joy :
Onward they pass—to th' Capitol repair,—
By one grave act, the Senators declare
The Empire his—by conquest and by birth,
With their consent, and by superior worth :
To him they all authority commit,
To him in mercy and in peace submit :
His justice grants all prisoners release,
He gives the word, and persecutions cease ;—
He smiles benignant on the Christian shrines,
All heathen honours he with scorn declines ;
His virtue sanctions what his power enacts,
While his example all the realm attracts ;
The high, the learned, the simple, and the low,
In thousands flock their gratitude to show ;—
Embrace his faith—pay the baptismal vow,—
In humble reverence to the Cross they bow ;
Receive the Gospel's truth without research,—
Triumphant now The Universal Church. '

 END OF THE SIXTH BOOK.

---

[a] Page 141. Neither the severe laws of the Emperor Hadrian, nor the punishment with which he so signally and so cruelly avenged the massacre committed by Barchochebas and his followers on the inhabitants of Cyprus and Cyrene, nor the concessions made by the two succeeding Emperors, Antoninus and Aurelius, could either restrain or conciliate the turbulent disposition and determined hatred of the Jewish nation, always impatient of the Roman yoke,—and the failure of the Emperor Julian to restore their Temple, whether such failure be ascribed to miraculous or natural causes, the effect will ever remain a proof of the truth of Prophecy.

[b] Page 142. Twice only is it recorded in the New Testament that "Jesus wept,"—once over the dead body of Lazarus (St. John, c. xi., v. 35), and again when he prophesied the fall of Jerusalem (St. Luke, ch. xix., v. 41).

[c] Page 143. The rapid growth of the Gospel may justly be compared to that of the vine, in the number and strength of its branches, as well as the value of its fruit; as its revival from those transient persecutions, as the historian Gibbon styles the cruelties the Christians suffered under the predecessors of Diocletian, from Nero downwards,—may be to the trodden grass.

[d] Page 143. The condemnation and sufferings of the Christians under Nero, as related by Tacitus (*Annals*, Bk. xv., sec. 44), is generally designated by ecclesiastical historians—ancient and modern—as the first of the ten persecutions, and that under Domitian as the second. It has been objected that these acts of despotic, tyrannical, and cruel Princes, do not constitute persecution for the Faith, inasmuch as they were accidental, or incidental to the Christians as perpetrators of enormous crimes—the first for setting Rome on fire, the second for conspiracy and treachery in the palace of the Emperor; more particularly as neither of these atrocities extended beyond the precincts

M

of the city. However this objection may be supported, it is evidently the manifestation of a spirit inimical to the Church, and written or intended to disparage the authority of the early Fathers.

ᵉ Page 143. Ephesus was the city of which Timothy was the first Bishop, and where he received his martyrdom, as Smyrna was that of Polycarp, the next in succession to the Apostles, who suffered, in extreme old age, with many other Christians, in the reign of Marcus Aurelius, (vide Eusebius' Eccl. Hist.) Tarsus was celebrated as the birth-place of St. Paul, and doubtless furnished her due proportion of martyrs.

ᶠ Page 143. Throughout the whole of Egypt, the city of Alexandria in particular, and in many of the cities of Syria and Palestine, the followers of Christ suffered in considerable numbers during the reigns of Trajan and the two Antonines.—Vide Eusebius' Eccl. Hist.

ᵍ Page 146. The martyrdom of Ignatius, second Bishop of Antioch, which took place at Rome at the latter end of the reign of the Emperor Trajan, is attempted to be here described, according to the manner which he himself seemed to predict, as he passed through the different provinces on his way to the Imperial City, and which is recorded in Eusebius' Eccl. Hist.

ʰ Page 147. The martyrdom of Cyprian, which took place at Carthage, of which city he was Bishop, more than a century later than that of St. Ignatius (that is, in the reign of Valerian), bears a striking contrast to its predecessor, both in the manner in which it was conducted, and in the feelings of the populace. In the first, the martyr was given to the wild beasts as a spectacle for their enjoyment, who cared little whether the victim was a Christian or a Pagan, so that their taste for sanguinary and brutal exhibitions was indulged;—the last was executed as a criminal, upon whom sentence had been passed after the custom of the Roman law, which had received the sanction of several of their Emperors; and amidst a concourse of friends and followers who manifested great grief at his death, without any interruption from the people or the military—a proof that in those early days Christianity had undergone a great change in public opinion, and was increasing to a surprising degree.

ⁱ Page 148. The cities of Lyons and Vienna, in Gaul, were

celebrated for the numbers and horrible sufferings of their martyrs of both sexes, particularly the slave Blandina.— *Vide* Eusebius' *Eccl. Hist.*, Bk. v., ch. i.

ʲ Page 148. As Alban, or Albanus, was the first martyr in Britain, and his execution not taking place till the year 303 as nearly as can be ascertained, this Island must have been exempt from the earlier persecutions; and indeed, according to some of the early writers, was one of those distant Provinces to which the accused or suspected fled for their lives, as well as for the more uninterrupted and open profession of their religion.

ᵏ Page 149. This description of Britain when under the rule of Carausius, who for a time dismembered it from the Roman Empire, and under Constantius Chlorus, who recovered it, is attested by the early writers, though not fully assented to by Gibbon.

ˡ Page 150. The tenth and last persecution, under Diocletian, extended over the whole Empire, but fell heaviest in the Eastern Provinces, under the vindictive rule of Maximian and Galerius. One town in Phrygia was burnt, with its garrison and inhabitants.— *Vide* Eusebius' *Eccl. Hist.*, Bk. viii., ch. xi.

ᵐ Page 150. The government of Constantius Chlorus, in the Western Provinces, was in every way serviceable to the persecuted Christians,—for although he could not oppose the edict of Diocletian, his known partiality for the sect induced his officers not to listen to the informers against them, or to take means to evade the law or mitigate the punishment,—while he himself took them under his especial care and protection, and recommended them and their cause on his dying bed to his son and successor Constantine.

ⁿ Page 151. It would be a difficult matter for the topographer to satisfy the inquiring mind as to the precise site of the decisive struggle between the army of infuriated Britons, headed by the injured and ill-fated Boadicea on the one hand, and the disciplined legions under Suetonius on the other. The text of Tautus, brief and recondite as it is, will help the diligent inquirer much to persuade himself that the narrow valley that separates the present town of St. Alban's from the remains of the ruins of the walls of the ancient Verulam, *is* the ravine where the Romans awaited the attack of their undisciplined adversaries : he must then, in his mind's eye, afforest the adjacent hills and the country through which they advanced, to the entrance of the ravine where Sopwell Nunnery once stood, the remains of which are still to be seen ; then following the ravine he would issue on the plain extending from St. Michael's church to Gorhambury, where he may reasonably conclude the great slaughter of the Britons took place ; as attested by spear-heads and other broken implements of ancient warfare, Roman and British coins, and other curiosities, which have been for years past, and are to this day, turned up by the plough. Taut. *Ann.*, Bk. xiv., secs. 34, 35, 36, 37. This battle or massacre took place in the year 61 ; the fire of Rome in the year 64, of the Christian era.

° Page 154. The martyrdom of St. Alban is peculiarly an English subject, either for the Poet or the Painter. If we could clear the original from the dust and dirt that a thousand years of ignorance and superstition had thrown over it, hardened, as it soon afterwards became, by monastic cupidity—if we could restore the picture, not with the harsh dry brush of sceptical animosity, or the not less destructive instrument of polemic rivalry, but with the soft warm unguents of kindred love and Christian brotherhood, we should behold a most beautiful manifestation of the Christian virtues. Faith, love, self-denial and fortitude, would then be exhibited in the full glow of those pristine colours, with which the conversion of a Briton, a man of rank and education, in the early ages of Christianity, when it was struggling with the powers of darkness, that stimulated earthly rulers to attempt its destruction,—had indelibly stamped it. The author has here endeavoured to extract from the legend or legends which have so disfigured the original, the simple narrative, of itself sufficiently interesting to every Englishman, who regards his faith, or honours the land of his birth, and can only regret that his feeble efforts have failed to give effect to the pathos so sublime a subject contains.

ᵖ Page 155. The personal appearance of the great Constantine is unanimously commended and recorded by all contemporary writers, and the beauty of his countenance is still attested by coins,—his character is drawn according to the tastes, the creed, the religious zeal, or the situation of the different writers, who perhaps took different stages of his life to exhibit his virtues or his vices. The eulogies and panegyrics of some are justified by his Imperial patronage of the Christian Faith, his clemency, his toleration, his humanity and his piety; his condemnation by others, for acts committed in a later period of his life and reign, is equally justified—for the execution of his son Crispus will ever remain a blot upon his profession as a Christian, and his rule as an Emperor.—See *Gibbon*, ch. xvii.

ᑫ Page 156. The defeat of the Franks beyond the Rhine occupied the arms and valour of Constantine, when his father-in-law Maximian conspired to depose him from the sovereignty of Gaul: the defeat and death of that Prince are minutely related by ancient authors, both Christian and Pagan.—See *Gibbon*, ch. xiv.

ʳ Page 157. The author has here attempted to describe the outward and visible signs of the dream, as being more compatible with his office and the manner he has treated the subject from the commencement, than to endeavour to give an account of the dream itself, for which the reader must refer to Eusebius' *Life of Constantine*, Lactantius, and other ancient writers.

ˢ Page 158. The date of the conversion of Constantine has been variously set down by the ancients—earlier or later, according to their love or hatred of the Emperor and his new religion—as the flattery of his friends or the vindictiveness of his enemies dictated: the author has placed it as immediately following the dream, which might have been (and circumstances seem to justify the supposition) a præternatural communication, as we have no proof that such means of conveying the will or intention of the Deity—(of which we have so many instances both in the Old and New Testaments)—had been discontinued; and it is more than probable, from the testimony of the ancients and other collateral evidence, that the Labarum, or new standard, was first used in the battle of the Milvian Bridge.

ᵗ Page 158. The celestial sign, or the vision of the Cross in the heavens, is almost unanimously attested by contemporary writers; but Mr. Gibbon, in the same vein that pervades his celebrated diatribe or satire on the Christian religion, contained in the 15th and 16th chapters of his great work, both disputes their authority and attempts to resolve it into a physical or imaginary occurrence. Be this as it may, all natural phenomena are under the controul and at the command of an omniscient and omnipotent Being ; and the effects of this singular appearance in the heavens went to establish the first Christian Emperor on the throne of the Cæsars.

" Page 160. The battle of the Milvian Bridge was decisive of the cause of Christianity and Paganism, as it was of the success and future fame of Constantine the Great.

' Page 160. The testimonies of all the ancient authors to the rapid spread of the Gospel that followed the conversion of Constantine have been judiciously condensed by Gibbon, ch. xv.

———————

The book from which the author has drawn the principal historical features of the last canto, or Book, of his Poem, has been a subject of frequent critical and angry discussion, as well as of praise and admiration, for now three quarters of a century. During that time, many learned Divines have condemned its author for an assumed or real hostility to Christianity. But hitherto critics and commentators, editors and apologists—English, French, and German—have failed to discover or to make known the springs of action, or motive, that could induce a man of such profound knowledge, possessed of such a vast reasoning capacity, to assail the established faith of so many nations and centuries.

On the first appearance of so forcible, though so covert an attack, conducted with so much skill and energy, Theologians, lay and clerical, men eminent for their ability and piety, flocked to the rescue. They have been followed in these later days by men of equal zeal and talent, who, instead of persisting in the charge of a rancorous animosity or downright infidelity, have endeavoured to palliate the offence, or excuse the offender, by mitigating his faults, or by a mild interpretation of his most objectionable remarks on the origin, infancy, and growth of our holy religion.

A youth whose education had been matured in France (or Switzerland), whose lively sensibilities had imbibed all the attractive and seductive qualities of the first writers and philosophers of that age and nation,—as evinced by his frequent reference, if not deference, to their opinions, and by his own assertion that Paschal and Montesquieu were the models by which he formed his principal weapon, Satire— as a man, confident in his power of wielding so fearful an instrument, scorning the lesser emanations of the human mind,—Mr. Gibbon concentrated all his efforts to attack with its poisoned point a Divine institution, as the one only worthy of his gigantic intellect. His reverence for the ordinances and ceremonies of religion had already been shaken by his early conversion and his speedy re-conversion, while the love of his subject and the admiration with which he viewed the monstrous fabric that had for so long a period held dominion over the fairest part of the globe, led him insensibly, in tracing its downfall, to the conclusion that the change of religion was one of the many causes, if not the principal one, that helped to undermine its foundation. This would further lead him to contrast the magnificence of the ancient form of worship with the too palpable poverty of the new,— the pompous procession of Ædiles and Priests of Jupiter with the shoeless and coarsely-clad followers of Christ,—a contrast upon which he could whet the edge of his weapon, and which would enable him to make his thrusts with more certainty and precision, and with greater gratification to his own immediate followers and admirers.

In thus attempting to assign a motive for what the great historian has been so loudly and so justly condemned, the author is unsupported perhaps by those high authorities that from position and education were better able to combat and rebut his insidious attacks on that religion of which they were, many of them, the ministers and legitimate defenders. Still the common wayfarer on the high road of life, unacquainted with, or unmindful of, the flowers of logic that lay in his path, would be unwilling to believe a mind so gifted as was that of the author of such an invaluable production—a mind completely furnished with all the attributes needful for such a task—a heart, too, that beat in unison with all the best feelings of our nature, undisturbed as it appears to have been by any remorse or repugnance of what might be the issue—could be impenetrable to the truth of the evidence of revelation. Vanity, or ambition, is inherent in our nature, from which the strongest mind and purest heart is not free, and to which most other human passions or mental acquirements are subservient. To surpass all others—in that golden age of science and philosophy, in which he says it was his good fortune to be born—in the use he made of that most striking quality or accomplishment of the human mind, was his principal aim ; and he exhibited his skill in a cause which many of his contemporaries had assailed with the more ponderous, but not more destructive weapons of ridicule and blasphemy. To this then, and not to a settled and determined hatred of our Faith, may be ascribed his strenuous but vain efforts to impeach its Divine origin, and which, like the spots on the sun, will ever partially deface one of the most brilliant, most instructive, and most useful compositions in the English language.

THE END.

PRINTED BY HENRY TUCK, 16 & 17, CLOTH FAIR, WEST SMITHFIELD, LONDON.